BIRNBAUM GUIDES

2011

Disney Cruise Line

Wendy Lefkon
EDITORIAL DIRECTOR

Jill Safro
EDITOR

Debbie Lofaso
DESIGNER

Jessica Ward
ASSISTANT EDITOR

Pam Brandon
CONTRIBUTING EDITOR

Lois Spritzer
CONTRIBUTING WRITER

Alexandra Mayes Birnbaum
CONSULTING EDITOR

THE OFFICIAL GUIDE

DISNEY EDITIONS

NEW YORK

For Steve Birnbaum, who merely made all this possible.

Additional text by Jill Safro

Cover photograph by Mike Carroll

All rights reserved. Published by Disney Editions, an imprint of Disney Book Group. No part of this work may be reproduced or transmitted in any form or by any means, electronic or mechanical, including photocopying, recording, or by any information storage and retrieval system, without written permission from the publisher. For information address Disney Enterprises, 114 Fifth Avenue, New York, New York 10011-5690.

ISBN: 978-14231-2376-7
V381-8386-5-10213

Printed in the United States of America

Other 2011 Birnbaum's Official Disney Guides:

Disneyland

Walt Disney World

Walt Disney World Dining

Walt Disney World For Kids

Walt Disney World Pocket Parks Guide

Certified Chain of Custody
Promoting Sustainable
Forest Management
www.sfiprogram.org
the SFI label applies to the text stock

A WORD FROM THE EDITOR

Birnbaum editors are notoriously proud of their knowledge when it comes to all things Disney. After all, we've been gathering expertise about Disney theme parks for more decades than we care to admit. But luxury ocean liners? Tropical islands? Foreign ports of call? These represented some seriously uncharted waters for us . . . until we created this, our annually updated official guide to Disney Cruise Line. After comprehensive, grueling (yeah, right) research, we happily boast expert status in this area, and we're eager to share what we've learned.

For starters, we quickly realized that a voyage with the Mouse is atypical in a number of ways. Most obviously, there's the simultaneous (and successful) catering to families with kids and grown-ups *sans* offspring. In fact, each ship has programming designed to draw young, old, and those in between to entirely different recreational areas. Then there's the innovative "rotational dining system," a lineup of lavish musical productions, deck-shaking dance parties with Disney characters, and, of course, the possibility of a unique grand finale: a full day at Castaway Cay—a private, almost-too-good-to-be-true tropical island.

Like swaying in a hammock in the aforementioned paradise, the idea of purchasing a vacation package may lull one into an "everything is taken care of" sense of security. The truth is, there are still dozens of decisions to make, staterooms to select, shore excursions to book, etc. Within these pages, as with any Birnbaum guide, you'll find detailed, accurate information meant to help you plan a successful vacation.

Of course, even with our rigorous research missions (which, incidentally, began with the inaugural sailing of the *Disney Magic* in the summer of 1998), this book would not exist without the contributions of so many. To begin with, we owe a big thank-you to the folks at Disney Cruise Line. Although all editorial decisions are made by the editor, it's their willingness to explain operations and provide factual data that makes this the Official Guide.

I'd like to extend a boatload of gratitude to Marcy Storm, Larry Stauffer, Jara Church, Kim Keller, Ana Fries, Maureen Landry, Erin Jackson, Dan Burklew, Shelley Gold-Witiak, Karen Bowman, and especially to Jonathan Frontado and Jason Lasecki for the care and effort that they have put into this project.

For their key roles behind the scenes, we salute Nisha Panchal, Jennifer Eastwood, Erika Nein, Michelle Olveira, Heather Pommerencke, Joan Peterson, and Mike Carroll.

Of course, no list of acknowledgments is complete without our founding editor, Steve Birnbaum, as well as Alexandra Mayes Birnbaum, who continues to provide gentle guidance and invaluable insight.

Finally, it's important to remember that specifics do change. To that end, we refine and expand our material with each annual revision. For the present edition, though, this is the final word.

Bon Voyage!

— Editor

WHAT DO YOU THINK?

Nothing is more valuable to us than your comments on what we've written and on your own experiences with Disney Cruise Line. Please share your insights with us by writing to:

Birnbaum's Official Guide to Disney Cruise Line, 2011
Disney Editions
114 Fifth Avenue, 14th Floor
New York, NY 10011
Attn: Jill Safro

TABLE OF CONTENTS

BEFORE YOU SAIL

Read this and you'll have everything you need to know before you go—Disney Cruise Line itineraries, how to select a cruise package, stateroom specifics, packing pointers, and much more.

ALL ABOARD

This deck-by-deck view of the *Disney Magic*, *Disney Wonder*, and the brand-new *Disney Dream* takes you on a stem-to-stern tour, starting with check-in and finishing with a visit to the spa. By the time you board, the ship should feel like home.

PORTS OF CALL

Here's a brief background about ports visited by Disney Cruise Line, peppered with information about Bahamian and Caribbean shore excursions, plus our first-hand accounts, to help you choose which shore tours to take and which you can skip.

LAND AND SEA VACATIONS

Can't decide between a stay at Walt Disney World or a voyage aboard Disney Cruise Line? Why not combine the two? This chapter explains how to get the most out of a "land and sea" vacation package.

BEFORE YOU SAIL

Planning Ahead

The fact that you are holding this book means that you have probably decided to make Disney your cruise vacation choice. Now comes the hard part: Which cruise package is best for you? How do you book it? What should you do to prepare for the voyage? The chapter that follows should answer these questions and help—whether this is your first cruise or your 50th—make the idea of a Disney Cruise reality.

Selecting a Cruise

What to do, what to do. There are many factors to consider when choosing a cruise package. Among the most important are destination, budget, time available, stateroom needs, and preferred itinerary.

If you want to take the most inexpensive cruise possible, then a 3-night cruise in a standard inside stateroom is probably a good choice. If money is no object, consider a 7-night adventure in the super-deluxe Walt Disney Suite. Of course, there are plenty of things in between—including pairing a Disney Cruise with a stay at Walt Disney World (see page 204). As for itineraries, there is a multitude of options from which to choose. What follows is a rundown of the itineraries that were most widely offered at press time.

ITINERARIES*

3-Night Bahamian Cruise

DAY	ITINERARY
Thursday	Check in at Port Canaveral Terminal. Aboard by 4 P.M.
Friday	Ashore at Nassau at 9:30 A.M. Aboard by 7 P.M.
Saturday	Ashore at Castaway Cay at 8:30 A.M. Aboard by 4:30 P.M.
Sunday	Ship at Port Canaveral beginning at 7:30 A.M.

4-Night Bahamian Cruise/Sunday Sailing

DAY	ITINERARY
Sunday	Check in at Port Canaveral Terminal. Aboard by 4 P.M.
Monday	Ashore at Nassau at 9:30 A.M. Aboard by 7 P.M.
Tuesday	Ashore at Castaway Cay at 8:30 A.M. Aboard by 5 P.M.
Wednesday	Full day at sea.
Thursday	Ship at Port Canaveral beginning at 7:30 A.M.

*Itineraries and times were correct at press time, but are subject to change for 2011.

4-Night Bahamian Cruise/Wednesday Sailing

DAY	ITINERARY
Wednesday	Check in at Port Canaveral Terminal. Aboard by 4 P.M.
Thursday	Ashore at Nassau at 9:30 A.M. Aboard by 7 P.M.
Friday	A full day at sea.
Saturday	Ashore in Castaway Cay at 8:30 A.M. Aboard by 4:30 P.M.
Sunday	Ship at Port Canaveral beginning at 7:30 A.M.

4-Night Bahamian Cruise/Friday Sailing

DAY	ITINERARY
Friday	Check in at Port Canaveral Terminal. Aboard by 4 P.M.
Saturday	Ashore at Nassau at 9:30 A.M. Aboard by 7 P.M.
Sunday	Ashore in Castaway Cay at 8:30 A.M. Aboard by 4:30 P.M.
Monday	A full day at sea.
Tuesday	Ship at Port Canaveral beginning at 7:30 A.M.

5-Night Bahamian Cruise
with Two Calls to Castaway Cay/Tuesday Sailing

DAY	ITINERARY
Tuesday	Check in at Port Canaveral Terminal. Aboard by 4 P.M.
Wednesday	Ashore in Castaway Cay at 8:30 A.M. Aboard by 4:30 P.M.
Thursday	A full day at sea.
Friday	Ashore at Nassau at 9:30 A.M. Aboard by 6 P.M.
Saturday	Ashore in Castaway Cay at 8:30 A.M. Aboard by 4:30 P.M.
Sunday	Ship at Port Canaveral beginning at 7:30 A.M.

5-Night Bahamian Cruise
with Two Calls to Castaway Cay/Sunday Sailing

DAY	ITINERARY
Sunday	Check in at Port Canaveral Terminal. Aboard by 4 P.M.
Monday	Ashore at Castaway Cay at 8:30 A.M. Aboard by 4:30 P.M.
Tuesday	Ashore at Nassau at 9:30 A.M. Aboard by 6 P.M.
Wednesday	A full day at sea.
Thursday	Ashore at Castaway Cay at 8:30 A.M. Aboard by 4:30 P.M.
Friday	Ship at Port Canaveral beginning at 7:30 A.M.

7-Night Western Caribbean Cruise

DAY	ITINERARY
Saturday	Check in at Port Canaveral Terminal. Aboard by 4 P.M.
Sunday	Ashore at Key West at 12:30 P.M. Aboard by 7:30 P.M.
Monday	Full day at sea.
Tuesday	Ashore at Grand Cayman at 7:30 A.M. Aboard by 4:30 P.M.
Wednesday	Ashore in Cozumel at 9:45 A.M. Aboard by 6:30 P.M.
Thursday	Full day at sea.
Friday	Ashore at Castaway Cay at 9:30 A.M. Aboard by 4:30 P.M.
Saturday	Ship at Port Canaveral beginning at 7:30 A.M.

7-Night Eastern Caribbean Cruise

DAY	ITINERARY
Saturday	Check in at Port Canaveral Terminal. Aboard by 4 P.M.
Sunday	Full day at sea.
Monday	Full day at sea.
Tuesday	Ashore in St. Maarten at 7:45 A.M. Aboard by 6:30 P.M.
Wednesday	Ashore in St. Thomas at 7:45 A.M. (It's possible to experience excursions to St. John, too.) Aboard by 3:45 P.M.
Thursday	Full day at sea.
Friday	Ashore at Castaway Cay at 9:45 A.M. Aboard by 4:30 P.M.
Saturday	Ship at Port Canaveral beginning at 7:30 A.M.

7-Night Mediterranean Cruise

DAY	ITINERARY
Saturday	Check in at Barcelona, Spain, terminal. Aboard by 4 P.M.
Sunday	Ashore in Villefranche, France, at 9 A.M. Aboard by 5:30 P.M.
Monday	Ashore in La Spezia, Italy, at 7:30 A.M. Aboard by 7:30 P.M.
Tuesday	Ashore in Civitavecchia, Italy, at 7:45 A.M. Aboard by 9 P.M.
Wednesday	Ashore in Naples, Italy, at 7:45 A.M. Aboard by 9 P.M.
Thursday	Full day at sea.
Friday	Ashore at Palma, Mallorca (Spain), at 7:45 A.M. Aboard by 6 P.M.
Saturday	Ship at Barcelona, Spain, beginning at 7 A.M.

7-Night Mediterranean Cruise with Cannes

DAY	ITINERARY
Saturday	Check in at Barcelona, Spain, terminal. Aboard by 4 P.M.
Sunday	Ashore in Cannes, France, at 7:45 A.M. Aboard by 5:30 P.M.
Monday	Ashore in La Spezia, Italy, at 7:30 A.M. Aboard by 7:30 P.M.
Tuesday	Ashore in Civitavecchia, Italy, at 7:45 A.M. Aboard by 9 P.M.
Wednesday	Ashore in Naples, Italy, at 7:30 A.M. Aboard by 9 P.M.
Thursday	Full day at sea.
Friday	Ashore at Palma, Mallorca (Spain), at 7:45 A.M. Aboard by 6 P.M.
Saturday	Ship at Barcelona, Spain, beginning at 7 A.M.

7-Night Alaska Cruise*

DAY	ITINERARY
Tuesday	Check in at Vancouver, Canada, terminal. Aboard by 3 P.M.
Wednesday	Full day at sea.
Thursday	Ashore at Tracy Arm, Alaska.
Friday	Ashore at Skagway, Alaska, at 7:15 A.M. Aboard by 7:30 P.M.
Saturday	Ashore at Juneau, Alaska, at 7:45 A.M. Aboard by 4:30 P.M.
Sunday	Ashore at Ketchikan, Alaska. Aboard by 7:30 P.M.
Monday	Full day at sea.
Tuesday	Ship at Vancouver, Canada, terminal beginning at 8 A.M.

*Information was correct at press time. For updates, visit *www.disneycruise.com*.

7-Night Mexican Riviera Cruise

DAY	ITINERARY
Sunday	Check in at Port Canaveral Terminal. Aboard by 4 P.M.
Monday	Full day at sea.
Tuesday	Full day at sea.
Wednesday	Ashore in Puerta Vallarta, Mexico, at 7:30 A.M. Aboard by 7 P.M.
Thursday	Ashore in Mazatlán, Mexico, at 7:30 A.M. Aboard by 7:30 P.M.
Friday	Ashore at Cabo San Lucas, Mexico, at 7:30 A.M. Aboard by 7:30 P.M.
Saturday	Full day at sea.
Sunday	Ship at Los Angeles, California, terminal beginning at 9:30 A.M.

17

10-Night Mexican Riviera Cruise

DAY	ITINERARY
Sunday	Check in at Los Angeles, California, terminal. Aboard by 4 P.M.
Monday	Full day at sea.
Tuesday	Full day at sea.
Wednesday	Ashore in Puerta Vallarta, Mexico, at 7:30 A.M. Aboard by 10 P.M.
Thursday	Full day at sea.
Friday	Ashore at Manzanillo, Mexico, at 8:15 A.M. Aboard by 4:30 P.M.
Saturday	Full day at sea.
Sunday	Full day at sea.
Monday	Ashore in Mazatlán, Mexico, at 7:30 A.M. Aboard by 7:30 P.M.
Tuesday	Full day at sea.
Wednesday	Ashore at Cabo San Lucas, Mexico, at 7:30 A.M. Aboard by 7:30 P.M.
Thursday	Full day at sea.
Friday	Ship at Los Angeles, California, terminal beginning at 9:30 A.M.

10-Night Mediterranean Cruise

DAY	ITINERARY
Wednesday	Check in at Barcelona, Spain, terminal. Aboard by 4 P.M.
Thursday	Full day at sea.
Friday	Ashore in Valletta, Malta, at 8:30 A.M. Aboard by 6 P.M.
Saturday	Ashore in Tunis, Tunisia, at 8:30 A.M. Aboard by 4 P.M.
Sunday	Ashore in Naples, Italy, at 8 A.M. Aboard by 4:30 P.M.
Monday	Ashore in Civitavecchia, Italy, at 7:45 A.M. Aboard by 4 P.M.
Tuesday	Ashore at La Spezia, Italy, at 7:30 A.M. Aboard by 5 P.M.
Wednesday	Ashore in Ajaccio, Corsica, at 7:30 A.M. Aboard by 5 P.M.
Thursday	Ashore in Villefranche, France, at 8 A.M. Aboard by 7 P.M.
Friday	Full day at sea.
Saturday	Ship at Barcelona, Spain, beginning at 7 A.M.

Check Your Calendar

Determining the length of your cruise depends on several things—the first, how much time do you have in your busy schedule to devote to leisure? If your answer is only three or four days, don't despair: Disney Cruise Line has short cruises to the Bahamas, complete with a stop at Disney's own private island, Castaway Cay. If you have at least a week, you also have choices: 7- to 11-night cruises to the Caribbean, Alaska, the Mexican Riviera, and the Mediterranean. For updates, call 800-910-3659 or visit: *www.disneycruise.com.*

Check Your Checkbook

The cost of your cruise is the next issue on the planning board. Budgetary constraints can be eased in several ways: by taking one of the shorter cruises, choosing a less expensive cabin class, and by limiting the number of land tours and excursions you take at the various ports of call. Plan to eat aboard the ship, too—meals and snacks are included in every vacation package, as are many extras, including stage shows, movies, tours, lectures, games, bands, deck parties with characters, and more.

THE DREAM JOINS THE TEAM!

The *Disney Dream*'s inaugural voyage, in January 2011, brings the total number of ships in Disney Cruise Line's fleet to three. While similar to its sister ships in many ways, the new kid on the block is bigger, has more restaurants and bars, and has more stateroom categories than its predecessors. At press time, the *Dream* was expected to spend most of 2011 based out of Port Canaveral, along with the *Magic*, while the *Wonder* will take guests on West Coast sailings.

DISNEY CRUISE LINE RATES*

LENGTH OF CRUISE	ITINERARY	RATE RANGE
⚓ 3 nights	Nassau/Castaway Cay	$299–$4,749 (adult) $209–$1,299 (child age 3–12) $164–$709 (under age 3**)
⚓ 4 nights	Nassau/Castaway Cay	$399–$6,539 (adult) $249–$1,399 (child age 3–12) $184–$759 (under age 3**)
⚓ 7 nights	Caribbean, Mexican Riviera, or Alaska	$639–$7,669 (adult) $439–$2,419 (child age 3–12) $299–$1,289 (under age 3**)
⚓ Other itineraries	Pricing was not available at press time. For details, call 800-910-3659 or visit *www.disneycruise.com*.	

* Prices do not include tax and were accurate at press time—but may change at any time. Expect them to increase during the year. Package options may be added and/or altered.

** Babies younger than 12 weeks are not permitted to travel.

DID YOU KNOW?

The 1,367 miles of cable onboard would be enough to run an extension cord between Texas and Michigan.

WHAT'S NOT INCLUDED

Rest assured that all of your basic vacation
needs are covered by the "all-inclusive" price of
the cruise. However, there are always "extras" that
you may want to ante up a little cash for. Here's a
list of items and services that carry an extra charge:

- ⚓ Babysitting (See pages 36 and 98)
- ⚓ Port Adventures (aka shore excursions)
- ⚓ Expenses incurred while on land in ports of call (with the exception of food and most soft drinks at Castaway Cay)
- ⚓ Tipping aboard the ship (See page 47)
- ⚓ Alcoholic beverages
- ⚓ Palo and Remy (Dining at these optional, exceptional, reservations-necessary, adults-only restaurants costs about $15 per person for dinner and brunch and $5 per person for high tea.)
- ⚓ Refreshments at Cove Cafe, Vibe, and any bar or lounge
- ⚓ Spa treatments
- ⚓ Arcade games
- ⚓ Photographs snapped by the ship's photographers
- ⚓ Internet usage (See page 43)
- ⚓ Cell phone usage (See page 44)
- ⚓ Ship-to-shore telephone calls (There is a sizable fee for all calls, incoming and outgoing. Calls within the ship are free.)

With the exception of non-Disney ports of call, all "incidental"
charges will be billed to your stateroom, provided that you leave a
credit card imprint upon check-in. It's a good idea to have some cash
on hand (we bring about $300, just in case), but there are few
chances to use it. Except for tips, cash isn't accepted on the ships.
Same goes for Castaway Cay, with the exception of the post office—
stamps must be purchased with cash. Most of the non-Disney port
shops accept major credit cards, and most accept U.S. currency.

Selecting a Stateroom

Sure, you'd like the largest suite on the ship. No question, you want the biggest verandah. And, of course, you absolutely must have a great view. But if that doesn't fit your budget, there are other appealing options. Consider this: Every stateroom boasts nautical decor, has ample closet space, a television, and a small safe. Inside staterooms are much less expensive and not much smaller than their outside counterparts; on the *Disney Dream*, they have virtual portholes (digital screens). On the other hand,

should you decide to splurge, know that there are concierge rooms (*Dream* only) and larger suites with private verandahs where you can sip a refreshing beverage and read the newest page-turner, periodically taking a moment to gaze at the sea.

Of course, there are other factors to think about when selecting a stateroom. How many people are in your party? Are you traveling with young children? Perhaps a Deluxe Stateroom would suit your family's needs. These accommodations have queen-size beds, bunk beds for the

WHAT'S IN A NAME?

A whole lot, when it comes to Disney Cruise Line accommodations. Here's a listing of the types of rooms, with the most cost-efficient first. Note that it is possible to request side-by-side staterooms, but it can't be guaranteed. For specifics on stateroom amenities, turn to page 63.

- ⚓ Standard Inside Stateroom
- ⚓ Concierge Family Ocean-view Stateroom with Verandah (*Dream*)
- ⚓ Deluxe Family Ocean-view Stateroom (*Dream*)
- ⚓ Deluxe Inside Stateroom
- ⚓ Deluxe Ocean-view Stateroom
- ⚓ Deluxe Stateroom with Navigator's Verandah (enclosed verandah)
- ⚓ Deluxe Stateroom with Verandah (open verandah)
- ⚓ Deluxe Family Stateroom with Verandah
- ⚓ 1-Bedroom Suite with Verandah
- ⚓ 2-Bedroom Suite with Verandah
- ⚓ Deluxe 2-Bedroom Suite with Verandah (*Magic* and *Wonder*)
- ⚓ Concierge 1-Bedroom Suite with Verandah (*Dream*)
- ⚓ Concierge Royal Suite with Verandah
- ⚓ Royal Suite with Verandah
- ⚓ Deluxe Family Ocean-view Stateroom with Verandah
- ⚓ Deluxe Ocean-view Stateroom with Verandah
- ⚓ Deluxe Ocean-view Stateroom with Navigator's Verandah (*Magic* and *Wonder*)

kids, and a split bath (see page 63). A curtained divider provides a bit of privacy. Of course, there's always the Walt Disney Suite and the Roy E. Disney Suite—so if money is absolutely no object, treat your crew to one of these thousand-square-foot homes away from home. No matter what your requirements are, chances are Disney Cruise Line can meet them.

How to Book a Cruise

In addition to using *www. disneycruise.com* or contacting Disney Cruise Line (800-910-3659), many guests book through travel agents.

PAYMENT METHODS

Cruise packages, as well as incidentals, gratuities, hotel bills, and deposits may be paid by credit card (Visa, MasterCard, JCB Card, American Express, Diners Club, Disney Visa, etc.), traveler's check, cashier's check, money order, cash, or personal

ALL GOOD THINGS . . .

How time flies when you're having fun. You blink and it's time to go home! Here are a few tips about the debarkation process.

The day before your return to the debarkation terminal, you'll receive an information packet that includes a set of colored luggage tags. The color coding designates the area of the terminal in which you can pick them up. Be sure to remove the original tags from the inbound trip before you put new tags on all bags. (Guest Services has extra tags.) You will also receive a U.S. Customs form when applicable. Hand this form in as you leave.

On the night before debarkation, you'll have to put all checked luggage outside your stateroom before 11 P.M. (Bags will be collected and delivered to a color-coded area at the terminal.) Keep valuables, clothing for debarkation, medications, tickets, passports, and other key documents with you. At your last dinner, your waitstaff will tell you where and when breakfast will be served the next morning. After breakfast, it's time to grab your belongings and leave the ship, taking all your happy memories and, quite possibly, the promise to return again soon. Of course, guests participating in onboard airline check-in don't have to claim bags until their plane lands at their home airport.

check. Personal checks must bear the guest's name and address, be drawn on a U.S. bank, and be accompanied by proper identification (a valid driver's license with photo or government-issued photo ID). Keep in mind that the final payment for a cruise package must be made *at least 90 days* before your vacation commencement date for packages less than 10 nights, and 150 days

WWW.DISNEYCRUISE.COM

We've done our best to provide accurate, current information regarding all things Disney Cruise Line. That said, rates, itineraries, excursions, and other specifics are subject to change. For more information or to book a cruise or excursion, visit the new and improved, interactive Web site: *www.disneycruise.com*. The site is one of the most comprehensive and user-friendly Web sites we have ever seen. This is also the place to go for updates on Disney Cruise Line's new ship: *Disney Fantasy*.

ahead for cruise packages that are 10 nights or longer. Final payment due date varies for special itineraries.

Payments sent via mail should be addressed to:

Disney Cruise Vacations
P.O. Box 277763
Atlanta, GA 30384-7763.

Payments sent via courier service (i.e., FedEx or UPS) should be sent to:

Disney Cruise Vacations
Bank of America
Lockbox Services
Lockbox 277763
6000 Feldwood Road
College Park, GA 30349
(407-566-3500).

DEPOSIT REQUIREMENTS

When you book a trip, you'll get a "due date" for a deposit. The deposit is $200–$400 per person for 5-night sailings or less, $250–$500 for a 6-, 7-, and 8-night cruise, and $600–$800 for cruises of 10 nights or more. Deposit amounts may vary for special itineraries. Reservations will be canceled if a deposit is not received by the deadline. (Packages booked within the final payment date get special instructions.)

CANCELLATION POLICY

Though cancellations may be made by telephone or by mail, we suggest the phone.

Fees paid for canceling depend on when that call is made. Generally speaking, the smallest fees are incurred when cancellations are made at least 45 days in advance. If a cruise is canceled less than 14 days ahead, you'll pay for the whole package. To avoid this sad fate, we highly recommend insuring your trip. For details, see page 30.

What to Pack

"Cruise Casual" is almost always the operative phrase with Disney. Shorts, T-shirts, sundresses, and the like are fine daytime wear. At dinnertime, casual takes on a more

HOT TIP

Guests who plan to arrive at Port Canaveral the night before setting sail might consider staying at one of these resorts on nearby Astronaut Boulevard:

• Country Inns & Suites by Carlson. Rates range from $89–$129, and there is a shuttle to the cruise terminal; 321-784-8500 or 888-201-1746.

• Residence Inn by Marriott. Rates range from $169–$199; 321-323-1100 or 800-331-3131.

formal meaning: Set aside the shorts and plan on slacks (jeans are okay, except at Palo and Remy) and a collared shirt for men, with real shoes, as opposed to those of the tennis variety. The same goes for women, while dresses are suitable, too. On 7-night or longer cruises, there is a semi-formal and a formal night. While some folks don black tie and sequins, it's not necessary to break out formal wear if you prefer a more casual look.

On these occasions, the *Personal Navigator* (see page 68) will tip you off as to the appropriate attire. Many guests pack pirate garb, too, in anticipation of Pirates IN the Caribbean party night (don't forget your puffy shirt!).

Bathing suits are a must, as are beach shoes, wraps, sunscreen, sunglasses, and hats. Some sundries, including shampoo, conditioner, and body lotion, are provided in your stateroom. Others are available for purchase, but the prices are steep, and the shops aren't always open (U.S. Customs limits the operating hours). Take an inventory of the products you'll need daily, and be sure to bring them with you. Here's a checklist of must-haves: passport, cash, film or memory cards, waterproof ID holder, prescription medication (in original containers), at least one "dressy" outfit, and comfortable shoes.

Pack a Day Bag

Guests may check in at the port and board the ship as early as 1 P.M., but your luggage may not arrive until 6 P.M. (though usually earlier). Keep in mind that you will have access to your stateroom throughout the day, along with most shipboard amenities, including all pools so pack your swimsuit in a day bag. This should serve as, or fit in, a carry-on, as checked bags will be out of your hands once you surrender them. (Day bags can't be larger than 9 inches by 14 inches by 22 inches, and do not count as part of the two-bag-per-passenger quota.) The bag should also include passport, valuables, breakable items, and anything else you'll need during those first hours onboard. Note that most airlines require that carried-on liquids be in 3.4-ounce-or-smaller containers and fit into a quart-size, clear, plastic zip-top bag.

Booking Shore Excursions

All prospective Disney Cruise Line guests receive an advance list of the tours and activities that are offered at each port of call, so it makes sense to sign up before you sail. Our *Ports of Call* chapter (see page 110) offers descriptions of many Caribbean and Bahamian excursions, along with a personal reaction. (Details on 2011 excursions for West Coast and other itineraries were not available at press time.) Cancellations or changes may be made up to three days before the start of the cruise to receive a full refund. After that, you pay whether you play or not.

Shore Excursions (also known as Port Adventures) are quite popular and tend to fill up early. To book yours, visit *www.disneycruise.com*. To make last-minute arrangements, visit your ship's Port Adventures desk. Note that excursions are not operated by the Walt Disney Company.

IDENTIFICATION PAPERS

Unlike a visit to Walt Disney World's Epcot, where it only feels as if you're leaving the country, in the case of a Disney Cruise Line vacation, you really do. Given that, you'll need to provide proper proof of citizenship when passing through Customs. U.S. government regulations related to passport requirements are subject to change. Therefore, all guests should have a valid passport for all cruises. Call 877-487-2778 or visit *http://travel.state.gov* for current requirements.

HOT TIP

You will always have to show your "Key to the World" card (Disney-issued stateroom key and ID) when disembarking or boarding the ship. Adults also need a government-issued photo ID (a passport is ideal).

INSURE YOUR TRIP

Nobody books a vacation expecting to cancel it—yet sometimes life intervenes and it's unavoidable. That's why we advise you to make travel insurance a part of your vacation budget. (We do.) The Disney Cruise Line Vacation Plan provides baggage, trip cancellation/interruption, and medical-expense coverage for the duration of the cruise. The cost is calculated per guest. At press time, rates were $59 for the first and second guest and $39 per additional guest for a 3-night cruise; $69 for the first two guests and $49 per extra guest for a 4-night cruise; $99 for the first two guests and $49 per extra guest for a 5-night cruise; $109 for the first two guests, $59 per additional guest for a 7- or 8-night cruise; and $189 for the first two guests and $99 per extra guest for a 10- or 11-night cruise. Call 800-910-3659 for rates for other cruises. All rates are subject to change. Here's an overview of what's covered:

⚓ Trip cancellation/interruption protection (for medical reasons or other specific issues)

⚓ Travel-delay protection (for additional travel expenses incurred by you due to covered travel delays)

⚓ Emergency medical/dental benefits for the duration of your cruise (includes transportation to the nearest appropriate medical facility)

⚓ Baggage coverage (for lost or delayed arrival of baggage)

⚓ A 24-hour hotline to help with replacement of lost travel documents or emergency cash transfers. (From the U.S., call 877-593-4988; outside the U.S., call 804-281-5700. The program ID number is 001000287.)

How to get to Port Canaveral

By Plane

Fly to Orlando International Airport. We like flights that are scheduled to arrive in the morning hours. Why? Because that lets you check in and board the ship as early as possible. If you get there on the early side, you can make a day of it. And, if your flight is delayed, you'll still have a shot at making it to the port before the ship sails. (When you book your cruise, ask about the check-in cutoff time. Don't be late!)

From the Airport

As you get off the shuttle and enter the main terminal (after a tram ride), proceed directly to the Disney Magical Express Welcome Center. It's on Level 1, Side B of the terminal. After your party has checked in, a Disney rep will direct you toward a motor coach. Don't worry about luggage. For guests with transfers, all bags bearing appropriate tags will be claimed by Disney and delivered to your stateroom. (If you are driving to the ship, refer to page 32.)

The details that follow apply to cruises departing from Port Canaveral, Florida. Specifics about West Coast and Mediterranean cruises were not available at press time. For information, call 800-910-3659 or visit *www.disneycruise.com.*

Disney Motor Coach

The bus trip from Orlando International Airport or a Disney World resort to Port Canaveral takes about 90 minutes (without traffic). While onboard, you can fill out paperwork (though it is best to do this ahead of time). There is a restroom onboard. Motor coach vouchers may be purchased with a cruise package.

Car Service

Noris Limousine and Florida Towncar offer friendly, reliable service between Orlando International Airport (MCO) and Port Canaveral. For rates, information, or to make a reservation with Noris Limousine, call 888-240-4533 or 407-891-7503, or visit *www.norislimousine.com.* For Florida Towncar, go to *www.floridatowncar.com,* or call 800-525-7246 or 407-277-5466. Reservations are necessary, and cancellations must be made at least 48 hours in advance. Disney Cruise Line's reservations department can take your car service request, too.

Automobile

Disney Cruise Line's Port Canaveral Terminal is located on the north side or "A" Cruise Terminals; 9155 Charles M. Rowland Dr., Port Canaveral, Florida, 32920. It's about a 60-minute drive from Orlando International Airport and from Walt Disney World. The outdoor parking facility, which is operated by the Canaveral Port Authority, accepts cash (U.S. currency), Visa, MasterCard, and traveler's checks *only*. Personal checks are not accepted. The cost to park is about $15 per night. Rates are subject to change.

From Orlando International Airport, take State Road (S.R.) 528 East (Beachline Expressway). Continue over the Indian River and the Banana River. Turn right onto S.R. 401, which will loop and head north over the channel locks. Stay in the right-hand lane and follow signs to the "A" Cruise Terminals. S.R. 528 is a toll road. (Note that S.R. 401 used to be known as A1A.)

If you are driving from Walt Disney World, take State Road 536 East to 417 (The GreeneWay). Follow 417 to S.R. 528 East (Beachline Expressway). At the fork in the road, veer right to stay on S.R. 528. Continue over the Indian and Banana rivers. Turn right onto S.R. 401. Stay in the right lane

TAG YOUR BAGS

After you book your cruise, you'll get a personalized packet of information in the mail. Included in this valuable envelope will be colorful luggage tags. We cannot overemphasize the importance of affixing these tags to the luggage you plan to check at the airport. Why? Once you say good-bye to your bags at the airport, you won't see them again until they arrive at your stateroom. Magic? No, just a smooth operating system. Disney reps collect bags at baggage claim and deliver them to your stateroom by 6 P.M.

If you arrive by car or bus, drop your bags with porters at the terminal. They will be delivered to your stateroom for you.

You'll use a similar color-coding method to claim your bags on the final morning of your cruise. A new set of tags will be left in your stateroom. Slap the new tags on your bag, make a note of the color, and place them in the hall by 11 P.M. on the last night of the cruise. Look for them in the designated section of the terminal once you debark. *Guests participating in onboard airline check-in don't have to claim their bags until their plane lands at their home airport. Certain restrictions apply.*

COLD AND FLU ADVISORY

Disney Cruise Line follows extraordinary sanitation efforts to ensure the safety and comfort of guests. Even so, people can get sick. If you or a member of your party experience any symptom of illness (cold, flu, etc.) within 72 hours of sailing, you will be asked to postpone your trip. (Disney Cruise Line reps will direct you to someone who will help your party make alternative plans.)

Once onboard, all guests are asked to wash their hands frequently and thoroughly—as this is a highly effective barrier to spreading germs. If you or someone in your party does become ill during your trip, head directly to the Medical Center. You'll be taken care of there, and immediate treatment will help limit the potential impact to others.

and follow signs to the "A" Cruise Terminals. Note that 417 and 528 are toll roads.

Guests who are driving from North Florida should take I-95 South exit #205 for S.R. 528 East (Beachline Expressway). Continue over the Indian and Banana rivers. Turn right onto S.R. 401. Stay in the right lane and follow signs to "A" Cruise Terminals.

Drivers originating in South Florida should take I-95 North. Exit at #205 for S.R. 528 East (The Beachline). Take S.R. 528 to S.R. 401. Stay right and follow signs to "A" Cruise Terminals.

IMPORTANT NUMBERS
• Disney Cruise Line reservations and information: 800-910-3659
• Walt Disney World Central Reservations: 407-934-7639

Getting to Port Canaveral from WDW (without a car)

Disney Cruise Line has dedicated buses to chauffeur guests directly from most Walt Disney World resorts, except Fort Wilderness and the Swan and Dolphin. One-way transfers cost $35 per person, while $69 will cover the round trip. Guests will receive a letter in their resort room with departure details. Bell services will automatically pick up luggage when transfers have been pre-arranged. (Car services make the trip to and from the port, too. See page 32 for contact information.)

room. (The cribs are 39.8 inches long, 28.25 inches wide, and 31.25 inches high.) Request one when you make a reservation, and confirm it before leaving home. (If you booked your cruise package through a travel agent, call said agent with requests such as this.) Supplies are limited. Bring your own baby blanket, as the cribs come with fitted sheets only.

Customized Travel Tips

Traveling with Babies

CRIBS

If you are traveling with a baby, it is possible to have a playpen-like, foldaway crib sent to your state-

DIAPER SERVICE

It is possible to have a disposable diaper system sent to your stateroom. Request one when you make a reservation or speak with your Stateroom Host upon arrival.

LIGHTEN YOUR LUGGAGE

Traveling with an infant or toddler? Life just got easier for you! It's now possible to order baby supplies online and have them delivered directly to your stateroom. This Disney Cruise Line-exclusive is provided by Babies Travel Lite and offers more than 1,000 brand-name products (diapers, baby food, formula, etc.) Access the service by visiting *www.disneycruise.com*.

FOOD

Staterooms on the *Magic* and *Wonder* have a small "beverage cooler," which maintains a temperature of approximately 55 degrees. Formula and food can be stored safely within the unit. (*Disney Dream* staterooms have small refrigerators.) At least one shop onboard sells diapers, formula, and a small selection of food. (The shop isn't always open, as U.S. Customs limits its hours.) If you'd like to save money, pack as many baby rations as possible. Round-the-clock room service means you will never get caught with a screaming, hungry little one and no means of quelling the hunger pangs. Note that homemade baby food is not allowed onboard.

BABYSITTING

Onboard babysitting is available for tots ages 12 weeks to 3 years. The cost is

$6 an hour for the first child, with a one-hour minimum. Each additional child (who must be a sibling) is $5 per hour. The service is offered in the ship's nursery. Reservations can be made at *www.disneycruise.com* or onboard (based on availability). In-room babysitting is not offered on any ship.

OTHER SUPPLIES

Diapers, pacifiers, pool toys, and more can be purchased onboard. The shops aren't always open, so take inventory to avoid being caught short. If it's an emergency, inquire at Guest Services. They can help with just about any onboard crisis.

Travelers with Disabilities

Measures have been taken to make your stay as comfortable and effortless as possible. Each ship has staterooms that are equipped for guests using

MEDICINE STORAGE

All staterooms on the *Dream* have a mini fridge (perfectly suitable to storing medicine), but staterooms on the *Magic* and *Wonder* have a "beverage cooler." They are fine for storing food, but not necessarily medication (especially if it requires a stable temperature). Guests who need to store medicine should visit the ship's medical center, Guest Services, or request a small refrigerator. Availability is limited, so ask for one at the same time you reserve your cruise package. Call to confirm it before you leave.

HOT TIP

There is a small number of wheelchairs to borrow for use onboard, but if you'll be using a wheelchair for the entire trip (including ports of call), you should bring your own.

GETTING AROUND IT

Disabled travelers already know that travel requires a lot of advance planning. Disney has equipped its ships with a variety of amenities geared toward those guests with special needs.

Wheelchair-accessible staterooms are equipped with ramp entrances to bathrooms, fold-down shower seats, handheld shower heads, lowered towel and closet racks, a bathroom phone, and Emergency Call buttons.

There is a limited number of sand wheelchairs available (first come, first served). Note: If you will need a wheelchair throughout the cruise, you are encouraged to bring your own.

Throughout the ship, there are signs indicating the location of wheelchair-accessible restrooms.

Hearing-impaired guests need not miss any of the fun onboard. In-cabin TVs can be equipped with closed-captioning, and assisted-listening devices are available at all theaters and show rooms. Also available are communication kits equipped with strobe-light smoke alarms, door-knock and telephone alerts, and TTY (a text typewriter). Make your needs known when you book your cruise.

wheelchairs. They have ramped bathroom thresholds, open bed frames, bathroom and shower handrails, fold-down shower seats, handheld showerheads, and lowered towel and closet bars. Closed-captioning is available for stateroom televisions and for some onboard video monitors. Stateroom communication kits may be reserved upon request. They include door-knock and phone alerts, phone amplifier, bed shaker notification, a strobe-light smoke detector, and a text typewriter (aka TTY). There is no extra charge for the kit, but supplies are limited. Request it when you make your reservation and confirm it prior to sailing.

Wheelchair-accessible restrooms are available in several common areas onboard the ship. There are transfer tiers at the Quiet Cove pool. (Each is a multistep tier and is not

automatic. To use it, guests must be able to lift themselves out of their chairs.) Sand wheelchairs are available at Castaway Cay. American Sign Language interpretation is available for live performances on select cruise dates. (The service is not available on every cruise, so be sure to start planning your trip well in advance.) For additional information or to make special requests, ask your reservationist. For more information via TTY (text typewriter), call 407-566-7455.

Travelers without Children

This being a Disney cruise, one could argue that you—the footloose, fancy-free folks—are on their turf. And, as such, you might expect to have youngsters underfoot at all times. This is simply not the case. The Disney ships

were designed with three specific types of vacationers in mind: families, kids, and grown-ups without kids. Onboard, there is an adults-only deck area, complete with its own pool (not to mention music and games). There's a gourmet restaurant and a cozy coffee bar. It goes without saying that those spots, as well as several lounges, are strictly for the grown-up set (as in adults with legal proof of age). Plus, there are countless other ways to enjoy a grown-up getaway in the various ports of call. With that in mind, Castaway Cay (Disney's private island) guarantees you and your ilk a piece of beachfront real estate where you can bask in the sun or read a novel in the shade without the fear of sand being kicked in your face. You can even have a massage in a cabana overlooking the ocean.

Can you manage to spend days on end without encountering the wee ones of our species? No way. But who'd want to?

Medical Matters

The Medical Center, located forward on Deck 1, is open daily to assist with any medical emergencies or health concerns. Regular hours are from 9:30 A.M. to 11 A.M. and from 4:30 P.M. to 7 P.M. All Disney ships have a physician and nurse on call 24 hours a day (even while in port) for conditions requiring immediate attention. Health services are provided by a company independent from Disney Cruise Line, and standard prevailing fees will be charged for all services. Fees will be charged to your stateroom account.

In extreme cases, Disney Cruise Line will arrange to have a passenger taken to the nearest port to receive medical care.

The cost of this varies with the location of the ship and the nearest port. Because all health care provided qualifies as "care outside the United States," you will be responsible for paying any charges incurred while onboard prior to debarkation and submitting the request for coverage to your insurance carrier (paperwork will be provided).

If you get sick while on shore, your guide should direct you back to your ship's tour director at the dock, who will help you get back to the ship.

If you are a diabetic using insulin or take other medication that needs to be refrigerated during your

IT'S NOT EASY BEING GREEN

Unfortunately, Mother Nature being predictably unpredictable, the seas are occasionally a tad turbulent. So, there's always the possibility that you or a member of your party may become a little green about the gills. Plan ahead. We recommend packing a supply of over-the-counter medication (but know these may make you drowsy). We also suggest you pack ginger pills (available at most health food and vitamin stores) and drink ginger ale.

If you've experienced motion sickness in the past, try to steer clear of inside cabins (though the virtual portholes on the *Dream* may help). Outer cabins have windows—and the view of the horizon can be a helpful stabilizer. If the room has a verandah, all the better. Fresh air may not be an antidote to nausea, but it can't hurt. Some find relief in the form of bitters mixed with water or club soda. Then there are sea bands. They fit snugly around the wrist, supposedly alleviating symptoms by hitting key pressure points. You can pick them up at many pharmacies.

The good news is, most people get their "sea legs" very quickly, adjusting to the motion (slight or otherwise) soon after setting sail.

cruise, you can arrange for a small refrigerator to be brought to your cabin. Make your needs known well in advance. Take a supply of all prescription medicines with you, as the ship does not have a pharmacy. (Always travel with medicines in their original containers.)

Regarding younger passengers, know that a child exhibiting symptoms of illness will not be allowed to participate in youth activities or be cared for in the ship's nursery.

Special Occasions

For many travelers, taking a cruise is a special occasion in and of itself. Still, lots of folks choose to celebrate birthdays, anniversaries, and other special events onboard. If you fall into this category, be sure to tell your travel agent or alert Disney Cruise Line three weeks before you sail. That will ensure that your dining room staff will acknowledge your happy occasion over dinner. Some occasions, such as weddings and reunions, require a bit more preplanning.

Weddings

Whether you are saying your "I do's" for the first time, committing yourselves to one another, or renewing your vows, Disney Cruise Line has the means to make the occasion exceptionally memorable. Ceremonies may be performed on the ship or at Castaway Cay. Some happy couples invite family members along

for the trip, while others prefer to have this time to themselves. For more information, contact a Disney wedding consultant at 407-828-3400, or call your travel agent. Call as far in advance as possible.

Fingertip Reference Guide

Business Services

Wait a minute, aren't you here to relax? For those of you who must get a little work done while at sea, there are some business services available for an additional charge. Among them are fax transmission, copies, and AV equipment. There is Internet access (for a fee) at the Internet Cafe (adjacent to Promenade Lounge on the *Magic* and *Wonder*), the Cove Cafe (all ships), and in the conference facilities on the *Dream*; staterooms have phones (ship-to-shore rates apply); and electrical outlets are

laptop friendly. Note that the ships' computers are not equipped to accept uploads. There is, however, a handy printer at the ready. Ship-wide wireless Internet service is available (for a fee) to guests with wireless-ready laptops.

Camera Needs

By all means, bring a camera. Film and memory cards are sold onboard and at many ports of call. Keep in mind that undeveloped film should be packed in a carry-on bag, or risk having it destroyed by airport scanners.

There are also many

HOT TIP

If you were hoping to treat Fido to a high-seas adventure, think again. With the exception of service animals, Disney Cruise Line enforces a strict "humans only" policy. You will not be permitted to board with a pet of any kind.

Disney Cruise Line guests may be contacted by calling 888-322-8732 from the U.S. The international number is 1-732-335-3281. Ship-to-shore telephone rates apply. Those rates range from about $7 to $9.50 per minute. Callers should have the ship name and the name of the party they are contacting. To specify the ship, they would select 1 for the *Disney Magic*, 2 for the *Wonder*, or 3 for the *Dream*. Payment may be made by credit card. Messages can be recorded via voice mail.

Some guests may also be reached by personal cell phone. Wireless service, available in staterooms only, is available to subscribers of a host of cellular providers worldwide. Rates vary.

HOT TIP

If you plan to use your cell phone during your cruise, be sure to check with your wireless provider before leaving home. Ask if you'll get service through them while onboard and how much the service costs.

Disney photographers on the ship, capturing moments throughout the day. You'll find shots taken at "static locations" (i.e., character sets in the lobby) are available for viewing at photo kiosks outside Shutters (the ships' photo store) and by the Promenade Lounge on the *Magic* and *Wonder*. Unlike with the PhotoPass system at Walt Disney World, these photos may only be viewed and purchased during the cruise. Photos taken by roaming photographers (i.e., in the dining rooms, by the pool, on Castaway Cay, etc.) may be viewed and purchased inside Shutters. This is also the place to transfer digital photos from a memory card or stick to a CD (for a fee).

Drinking Laws
The drinking age on the ships is 21 and is

strictly enforced. Valid photo ID is required. Disney Cruise Line reserves the right to refuse alcohol sales to anyone.

Mail

Letters and postcards may be mailed from the post office at Castaway Cay. Stamps are the only things available for purchase here (cash only). It's also possible to mail items from other ports of call—it's just a little less convenient. If you plan to mail anything from the Castaway Cay post office, do so early in the day. The closer it gets to 3:30 P.M., the longer the stamp line tends to grow.

Money Matters

There is no real need for cash on the ship. When you check in, an imprint of your credit card will be taken.

(Among the cards accepted are Visa, American Express, JCB Card, MasterCard, Discover, Disney Visa, and Diners Club.) From then on, all you'll need to do is sign for extras you want (including excursions booked on the ship), and these amounts will be charged to that card.

Cash or credit cards will be necessary for meals, taxis, and other purchases made in all ports except for Castaway Cay, as well as for postage at Castaway Cay. A few hundred dollars should suffice. Gratuities may be pre-paid, charged to a stateroom, or presented as cash placed in special envelopes. (See page 47 for tips on tipping.)

Automated teller machines may be available in ports of call, but there are none on the ship. Before using one, make sure it dispenses the type of currency you need.

45

SHIPBOARD AMENITIES

Here's a rundown of some of the less obvious amenities provided by Disney Cruise Line. (Charges apply.)

- ⚓ Complete laundry, dry cleaning, and valet services

- ⚓ Photo center that processes photos in an hour and has camera and video recorder rentals

- ⚓ Self-service launderettes

- ⚓ Satellite phone service

- ⚓ Internet cafe (*Magic* and *Wonder* only)

- ⚓ Wireless Internet service (available in many public spaces. BYO laptop.)

- ⚓ Modern medical facilities with a doctor and nurse on call

- ⚓ Stroller rentals

- ⚓ Telefax and secretarial services (on request)

- ⚓ Conference facilities for groups of up to 120 (*Wonder* only)

Smoking

Disney ships are, for the most part, smoke-free zones. All staterooms (including verandahs), lounges, restaurants, corridors, and most other areas are entirely nonsmoking. Smoking is only permitted at designated areas on the starboard side of open-air decks.

Telephone Calls

All staterooms have phones with ship-to-shore capability. Rates range from about $7– $9.50 per minute (subject to change). Toll-free and collect calls can't be placed from ship phones. Wireless service is available in staterooms. Be sure to check with your wireless carrier for rates. (See "How to Call the Ship" on page 44.) Some ports have pay phones, for which you'll need an international calling card.

Tipping

Some servers, such as bartenders and room service attendants, get an automatic 15 percent gratuity each time you call upon their services. Leave more if you deem the service to be outstanding. That said, folks such as your dining room servers and stateroom host or hostess do not receive any automatic gratuity. You have the option of pre-paying when you reserve your cruise (this helps expedite matters when the cruise comes to a close), or providing gratuities at the end of your trip. If a server goes above and beyond, you may add more than the standard 15 percent. Conversely, if he or she doesn't live up to expectations, you may reduce the amount (this situation has never happened to us). You can charge gratuities to the stateroom (at Guest Services) or pay with cash. Envelopes and receipts are provided. Hand envelopes to their respective recipients on the last night of your trip.

The chart below is a guideline as to how much you should give to whom:

PER GUEST/ PER CRUISE	3-NIGHT	4-NIGHT	5-NIGHT	7-NIGHT	10-NIGHT	11-NIGHT
Dining Room Server	$12	$16	$20	$28	$40	$44
Dining Room Assistant Server	$9	$12	$15	$21	$30	$33
Dining Room Head Server	$3	$4	$5	$7	$10	$11
Stateroom Host/Hostess	$12	$16	$20	$28	$40	$44
TOTAL:	$36	$48	$60	$84	$120	$132

ALL ABOARD

The moment you cross the gangway, you'll realize this vessel is no ordinary home away from home. Step into the grand, three-story atrium, and, amidst the happy hubbub, your presence is made known in dramatic fashion—with a heartfelt announcement for all to hear. And so begins your high-seas adventure.

The *Disney Magic*, *Disney Wonder*, and *Disney Dream* rank among the world's finest ocean-going vessels. The ships are casually elegant and designed to capture the majesty of early ocean liners. They're equipped to satisfy most cruisers, with a mix of traditional seafaring diversions and classic Disney touches. Though some theming and entertainment vary from ship to ship, the accommodations and amenities are similar. As is the service, which is expertly provided by a cast of thousands (representing dozens of countries). All staterooms aboard the trio of ships are a cut above normal cruising quarters —with an average of 25 percent more space than industry standard. The ships were designed to lure families and grown-ups without offspring to entirely different recreational areas. So, cast aside any preconceived notions you may have about cruising, and expect the unexpected. And don't forget to bring a camera!

Checking In

No matter where it is they call home—be it Bangkok or Boca, all Disney Cruise Line guests begin their respective journeys by checking in at a port terminal. For information on ports in Los Angeles, Vancouver, and Barcelona, visit *www.disneycruise.com* or call 800-910-3659. Bahamas- and Caribbean-bound guests check in at the "A" Terminals at Port Canaveral. Guests choose from several different queues at check-in: concierge, Castaway Club (for repeat guests), general check-in (for U.S. and Canadian citizens, and ARC cardholders), and a queue may be dedicated to guests sailing with a Travel Visa.

Though no one may board the ship until 1 P.M., guests are welcome to arrive as early as 10:30 A.M. The terminal has restrooms and ample seating to relax in while waiting to board. There's also a nifty model

of the ship to give you a preview of the real thing. And, if little ones get antsy, there's lots of room for them to roam around, plus TVs that run continuous loops of Disney cartoons. Mickey Mouse and friends occasionally greet guests in the terminal, too.

Okay, we may have gotten ahead of ourselves. Before you can enter the main part of the terminal, all members of your party must go through a security checkpoint. It's a lot like airport security, so save the holey socks for the second day of your trip (you may be asked to remove your shoes, along with jackets, glasses, belts, etc.). Since kids must go through the security check, too, we recommend having snacks and games to entertain them while you wait (in case the line is more than a few minutes long). Once you've cleared security, head toward the check-in counter.

51

At the counter, you will be asked to present a valid passport for yourself and each member of your party (see page 29). This is also where you'll be asked for all of your completed cruise paperwork (which can also be completed via the Internet at *www.disneycruise.com* under the "My Online Check-in" section; be sure to print the forms and bring them with you) and a major credit card. This card will be the one to which all of your extra cruise expenses are charged. If you'd like to split expenses with another guest staying in your stateroom, it is possible to register two different credit cards. Once

the cruise begins, you'll use your stateroom key—aka Key to the World—card to make purchases and to open your stateroom door. The card also serves as ID for debarking and reboarding purposes. Without it, you can't do either. If you'd prefer that any member of your party not have charging privileges, advise a representative at check-in (or indicate your preference when you check in online).

Once the check-in process is complete, you'll be directed to a Boarding Pass Image Processing station. Simply present your Key to the World card and say cheese. After your photo is snapped and encoded on your card, take a peek at your watch. Is it before 1 P.M.? If so, sit back, relax, and wait for the cue to board. You could also use the extra time to register kids for shipboard

AHOY, MATEY!

Throughout the cruise, you may hear a few terms with which you're unfamiliar. To avoid confusion, here's a little nautical talk 101:

Aft—directional term meaning toward the back (stern) of a ship

Bow—the front of a ship

Bridge—the place from which the captain and helmsman navigate a ship and give orders

Buoy—a floating object used to mark a channel or something lying under the water

Deck—a platform stretching along a ship

Forward—a directional term meaning toward the front of a ship

Funnel—a large, hollow tube or pipe through which exhaust from a ship's engine can escape

Galley—the kitchen on a ship

Hull—the outer frame or body of a ship

Knot—the measure of a ship's speed. One knot is one nautical mile per hour.

Midship—referring to the area in the middle of a ship

Port—the left-hand side of a ship (facing forward)

Porthole—a window in the side of a ship

Starboard—the right-hand side of a ship (facing forward)

Stateroom—living quarters for passengers and crew onboard a ship (aka cabin)

Stern—the rear end of a ship

youth activities. If it's after 1 P.M., grab the kids and your day bags and head for the gangway. All aboard!

The Boarding Experience

After you slip through the entry portal, you'll enter a subdued hallway. This is where you may have your "pre-cruise" family photo taken by a Cruise Line photographer. Try to look as stressed out and haggard as possible. That'll make the "post-cruise" shots that much more enjoyable. (You can buy copies of this photo on the ship later that day or soon after.)

On the far side of the photo-op area, there's a door leading to a covered gangway. Cross that and you'll find yourself deposited smack-dab in the middle of the ship's grand lobby. A dramatic backdrop for a dramatic entrance.

Depending on the time (staterooms are usually ready by 1:30 P.M.) and your level of starvation, you may want to make a quick stop, change, and head to Parrot Cay or Topsiders (on the *Magic*), Beach Blanket

Buffet (on the *Wonder*), or Enchanted Garden or Cabanas food court (*Dream*) for lunch. The pools are usually open throughout the afternoon. If you arrive as the time nears 2:30 P.M., skip the stateroom stop and make a beeline for the nearest eatery serving lunch—it's usually served until 3:30 P.M. After that, a visit to the stateroom is imperative, as the mandatory safety drill is at 4 P.M. (For the drill on the safety drill, see page 67.)

After the safety drill, you must head back to your room to replace the life vests and prepare for the 5 P.M. "Adventures Away" Sail Away Celebration. If you've got an early dinner seating, this is the ideal time to change into your evening attire.

Finally, we simply cannot overemphasize the importance of making reservations for spa treatments and for Palo and Remy (adults-only restaurants) as early as possible. (It's best to book before the trip, via *www.disneycruise.com*.) Make last-minute spa appointments at the spa itself. For Palo, which begins accepting reservations at 1 P.M. on day one of the cruise, head for Rockin' Bar D (*Magic*), or WaveBands (*Wonder*), or The District (*Dream*). Reservations for the *Dream*'s Remy (upscale dining for grown-ups) may be made here, too. Plan to register children for youth activities in the terminal or soon after boarding (see pages 94–99 for details).

HOT TIP

If you or a member of your party misplaces a Key to the World card while onboard, head to the Guest Services desk on Deck 3. They can issue a new one (free of charge).

Ship Shape

The *Disney Magic, Wonder,* and *Dream* are equipped to satisfy even the most savvy of cruisers, with a mix of traditional seafaring diversions and unmistakable Disney touches. The ships' classic exteriors recall the majesty of early ocean liners. Guests enter a three-story atrium, where traditional definitions of elegance expand to include bronze character statues and subtle cutout character silhouettes along a grand staircase. Recreation areas are designed to draw families and kid-free adults to different parts of the ship. By day, fun in the sun alternates with touring, lunch, indoor distractions, and perhaps even a little bingo action. Evenings give way to sunset sail-away celebrations, ultra-themed dining experiences, and theatrical extravaganzas. What follows is a description of the ships'

accommodations, shops, restaurants, lounges, pools, entertainment, and more.

Decked Out

Here's the deck-by-deck rundown, from top to bottom (it covers the *Magic*, *Wonder*, and *Dream*):

Deck 13

On the *Dream*, you'll find the Edge (tweens hangout), Currents (cozy bar), and Goofy's Sports Deck.

Deck 12

On the *Dream*, this is the location of the Senses Spa & Salon (which extends to Deck 11), Meridian (adults-only bar), Palo, and Remy (both are upscale eateries for grown-ups). It's also the site of the popular Aquaduck water coaster.

Deck 11

On the *Magic* and *Wonder*, you'll find the teen club Vibe. Formerly known as The Stack and Aloft, respectively, Vibe is

57

a teens-only spot (see page 80). On the *Dream*, this deck houses Cove Cafe (coffee bar for adults), Cabanas (food court), Mickey's Pool, Quiet Cove Pool, Donald's Pool, Nemo's Reef, and Arr-cade.

Deck 10

The Wide World of Sports Deck (*Magic* and *Wonder*). We find it a perfect late-night place to watch the moon and stars. There's also a basketball court. And this is one of the best places to be during the sail-away party. (For more on the sports deck, see page 105.) Palo is here, too (all ships), as is Remy (*Dream*). For adults only, these dining spots offer fine cuisine and panoramic views.

Deck 9

Pampering, Disney style, can be enjoyed in the 10,700-square-foot Vista Spa & Salon (*Magic* and *Wonder*). At the spa, guests may experience a variety of soothing treatments in the new spa villas, as well as a little R&R on the outdoor verandah. Fitness-minded folk can get a one-on-one fitness consultation. There's a vast selection of exercise equipment, saunas, a steam room, and spa treatments. (For details, see page 108.)

Deck 9 is also where you'll find the *Magic* and *Wonder*'s three pools: Quiet Cove (for adults); Mickey's Pool (for kids), complete with a kids-only spiraling slide; and Goofy's Pool (for families). There are a few ping-pong tables, too. This deck is also home to Cove Cafe, Quarter Masters (arcade), Goofy's Galley, Pinocchio's Pizzeria, Pluto's Dog House, and Topsider (*Wonder*) or Beach Blanket Buffet (*Magic*).

Deck 5

Kids pretty much have the run of this deck. It is one of the largest dedicated areas of children's space afloat, with comprehensive, age-specific activities. (For more about kids' programs, see page 94.)

The Buena Vista Theatre is also located here on all ships—although the *Dream*'s version extends to Deck 4. (A full-screen

PRINCESS AUTOGRAPH SESSION

The excitement builds as kids and their parents gather in a line for the chance to add treasured signatures to their autograph books. Once per cruise, regals such as Cinderella, Snow White, and Princess Aurora make their entrance, and the parade begins. Young admirers file past—many dressed in princess outfits of their own—stopping to ask each Disney Princess for an autograph. Don't forget the camera. Note that cruise staff members are on hand to make sure the line keeps moving. Check the *Personal Navigator* to see which princesses are scheduled to appear, as well as for dates and times.

cinema with Dolby Sound and 3-D technology, it offers films every day, featuring Disney's animated classics and first-run releases. It hosts guest speakers on occasion, too.) On the *Dream*, Deck 5 is also home to a happening teen hotspot called Vibe.

Deck 4

Here you'll find Studio Sea, the Walt Disney Theatre, Shutters (photo shop), and Animator's Palate. This is also a lovely deck on which to enjoy a leisurely stroll, a jog, or a nice nap.

The Walt Disney Theatre is a grand venue that features one of the most sophisticated show settings at sea or on land. The formal theater boasts extraordinary lighting and technical facilities, and showcases up to three distinct Broadway-style productions (with a decidedly Disney touch)

during each cruise. On the *Dream*, this venue extends to Deck 3.

Animator's Palate is a cheerful restaurant that offers creatively prepared cuisine in a room that features a colorful master-piece of synchronized light and sound. For additional information on Animator's Palate, see page 71.

Deck 4 is also the place where you can find a cheery duo of shops selling Disney Cruise Line-themed clothing, character merchandise, collectibles, specialty items, jewelry, and sundries. (See page 101 for more details.)

Exclusive to Deck 4 on the *Disney Dream*: D Lounge (family lounge and nightclub) and The District (grown-ups-only entertainment zone). Among the offerings here: Skyline Bar, District Lounge, Evolution (dance club), Metro Pub (sports

bar), and Pink (elegant evening cocktail spot).

Deck 3

This is the place for dining and dancing on the *Magic* and *Wonder*: Beat Street (*Magic*) and Route 66 (*Wonder*) are adult-oriented evening entertainment districts that offer themed

GUEST SERVICES DESK

As much as we like to think this book has all the answers, chances are, questions will arise onboard. If so, head to the Guest Services Desk (Deck 3, midship). This is also the spot to go to secure extra copies of the *Personal Navigator* and color-coded luggage tags (for use on the last day of the cruise). Should you have any type of problem while onboard, bring it to their attention. More often than not, they will resolve the issue in a matter of minutes.

clubs (see page 88 for details). Rockin' Bar D (*Magic*) and WaveBands (*Wonder*) have themed parties and live bands—and don't forget the room's biggest attraction . . . bingo! Diversions is a sports bar; Radar Trap (*Wonder*) and Up Beat (*Magic*) are duty-free shops; Sessions (on the *Magic*) and Cadillac Lounge (on the *Wonder*) are casual yet sophisticated places to relax and listen to live piano music; and Promenade Lounge is a place to enjoy a drink and hear music (on the *Magic* and *Wonder*). Adjacent to the Promenade Lounge is the Internet Cafe. (The *Dream* does not have an Internet Cafe, but does offer wireless Internet access.) Also here is Parrot Cay (*Magic* and *Wonder*), an island-inspired restaurant serving tropical cuisine, and off the lobby is Lumière's, serving continental cuisine (on the *Magic)*. Lumière's

has a French flair and a beautiful mural of Disney's *Beauty and the Beast*. Its counterpart on the *Wonder*, Triton's, has an underwater-like setting of blues, greens, and purples. Guest Services is also on this deck on the *Magic* and *Wonder*—it's open 24 hours a day. The Port Adventures (aka shore excursions) desk is nearby.

On the *Dream*, Deck 3 has the Bon Voyage lounge and the Royal Palace restaurant.

HOT TIP

All rooms have small safes (big enough for most laptops). There is no charge. (Lock it with a stateroom key, and unlock it using the same key.)

Deck 2

All ships have staterooms on this deck. The *Magic* also has a special area: Ocean Quest, which has a scaled-down replica of the ship's bridge, complete with "windows" (an LED screen), that lets youngsters (ages 11–13) experience the view from the real bridge. It's also got a captain's chair and a simulation game that lets kids steer the ship. The *Wonder* has conference rooms on this deck. On Deck 2 on the *Dream*, you'll find Enchanted Garden—the ship's large, main restaurant.

Deck 1

This is where you will find the ship's Medical Center. There are some staterooms here, too.

Decks 1, 2, 5, 6, 7, and 8

Shipboard accommodations are spread over these decks.

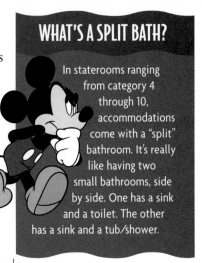

WHAT'S A SPLIT BATH?

In staterooms ranging from category 4 through 10, accommodations come with a "split" bathroom. It's really like having two small bathrooms, side by side. One has a sink and a toilet. The other has a sink and a tub/shower.

Staterooms

Also known as cabins, the accommodations range from standard inside rooms to suites with verandahs. All staterooms aboard each ship are a cut above the standard cruising cabin. On average, these staterooms offer about 25 percent more space, most have a bath and a half, and 73 percent are outside rooms with ocean vistas—many with verandahs.

Cabins are decorated in a

nautical theme with natural woods and imported tiles. Universal amenities include a TV, telephone with voice mail (and ship-to-shore capability), an in-room safe, a room service menu (in the Directory of Services book), and lots of drawer space. There's also a "cooling box." (It's chilly enough to store most perishables, but not medication.) After that, different types of accommodations—which are labeled by category— offer different amenities (verandahs are included in measurement of square footage):

CATEGORIES 11A–11C

Standard inside staterooms. They have a queen or two twin beds, a single convertible sofa, a privacy divider, and a bath. Each stateroom measures 184 square feet and sleeps up to 3 (category 11C) or 4 (categories 11A and 11B).

HOT TIP

The midship elevators are the most crowded throughout the day, but especially at mealtimes. Try to use the forward and aft elevators whenever possible.

CATEGORY 10A–10C

Deluxe inside staterooms. These accommodations are similar to those in categories 11A–11C, but have 214 square feet of space and a split bath.

CATEGORIES 9A–9D

Deluxe ocean-view staterooms. These come with a queen or two twin beds, a single convertible sofa, a privacy divider, and split bath. Rooms on Deck 1 have two small windows, while those on Deck 2 and above feature one large window. Each room is 214 square feet. It sleeps up to 3 or 4 guests.

CATEGORIES 5A–5C, 6A, AND 7A

Deluxe staterooms with verandahs. Each has one queen or two twin-size beds, a single convertible sofa, a privacy divider, split bath, and a verandah. These rooms are 268 square feet (including the verandah) and sleep up to 4. Category 7A has an enclosed "Navigator's Verandah," a private balcony with nautical touches. The verandahs in 5A and 6A are open (with the exception of staterooms located in the aft area). Accommodations are otherwise the same.

CATEGORY 4A, 4B, AND 4E

Deluxe ocean-view family staterooms. This room type has a queen or two twin beds, a single convertible sofa, and a bed that pulls down from the wall. There is a privacy divider, split bath, and open verandah

CHANNEL SURFING

Each Disney ship carries up to 21 different television stations. Rather than chastise you for watching TV when there's about a million better things to do onboard, here's a listing of the channels you can expect to find (some are commercial, some strictly in-house). Note that all channels are subject to blackouts:

Entertainment Guide
View from the Bridge
Bridge Report
Voyage Map
Shopping Channel
Slide/Discovery Travel
What's Afloat
Port Adventures/Debark Info
ABC/Discovery Channel
CNN Headline News
CNN
Slide/ESPN International
ESPN
ESPN 2
Disney Channel
Toon Disney
Music Video Channel
Shows from the Walt Disney Theatre
Company Clips
Disney Vacation Club
Sitcoms
Movies
Disney Animated Features

LAUNDRY FACILITIES

Laundry and dry-cleaning services are available for a fee. Items will be picked up and delivered to your stateroom. If you'd rather go the self-service laundry route, you can do so in one of several Guest Laundry Rooms. Here you'll find washers, dryers, and ironing equipment. (Due to safety concerns, the laundry room is the only place in which iron use is permitted.) There is no fee to use an iron. Machines run about two bucks a load. Laundry detergent may be purchased here, too. At press time, a small box cost $1. Simply swipe your Key to the World card and charge it to your room.

HOT TIP

Every day brings with it a new "drink of the day." It's a specialty cocktail served at the bars and lounges onboard. The beverage will be noted in the *Personal Navigator*. It is often available at a special price.

(verandahs in the aft area are not open). It covers 304 square feet (including verandah) and sleeps up to 5.

CATEGORY 00T

Concierge one-bedroom suites. These have a queen bed, an area with a double convertible sofa, and a pull-down bed (from the wall), two full baths, walk-in closet, unstocked wet bar, DVD player, open verandah (except for the aft-area staterooms), and concierge service. The suite is 614 square feet (including the verandah) and sleeps up to 4 or 5 guests.

CATEGORY 00S

Concierge two-bedroom suites with verandahs. These suites come with a queen bed, a sleeper-sofa, and a pull-down bed. There are 2.5 baths, a whirlpool tub, walk-in closets, a DVD

(Continued on page 68)

66

DAY ONE SAFETY DRILL

It's nearly 4 P.M. You've just started to unpack. You're weary from your journey. And all you want to do is plop down on a poolside lounge chair. Hold that thought. Before you get started on that much needed R&R, you've got a job to do. A very important, attendance-mandatory, skip-it-and-you've-broken-the-law job. It's called an Assembly Drill, and maritime law requires that all passengers participate prior to leaving your home port.

The drill is meant to prepare you for the unlikely event that you'd have to board a lifeboat. It sounds simple enough: Don your life jacket in your stateroom (they're on the top shelf of the stateroom closet and come in adult, child, and infant sizes), follow the signs to your assembly area, listen closely to the safety instructions, and shout out, "here!" when your stateroom number is called. But, believe it or not, some folks tend to wrestle with that life jacket for quite some time before figuring out just how to get that perfect, snug fit. And we don't want to tell you how lost we got on our way to our assembly station. That said, you might want to do a practice run. This way, when roll is called, your room can get checked off right away—and you won't have to postpone fun any longer than absolutely necessary.

Once the drill is completed (figure about 20 minutes), head directly back to your cabin to place your life jacket in its proper storage spot. Do not remove the jacket before you get to your room (though you will be tempted). Why? The straps on the jacket tend to wreak havoc with the pedestrian traffic on the stairs (the elevators do not operate during the drill). So, keep that jacket on—or risk a 50-passenger pileup.

FYI: The Disney Cruise Line safety drill has been rated number one by the United States Power Squadrons, a nonprofit organization dedicated to making boating as safe as possible. Good to know!

67

(Continued from page 66)

player, unstocked wet bar, private verandah, and concierge service. The suite measures 945 square feet and sleeps up to 7 guests.

CATEGORY 00R

Concierge royal suite with verandah. Comes with a queen bed in one bedroom, two twin beds in a second bedroom, and two ceiling pull-down upper berths. There are 2.5 baths, a whirlpool tub in the master bedroom, a living room, media library (with a pull-down bed), dining salon, pantry, unstocked wet bar, walk-in closets, DVD player, private verandah, and concierge service. The suite measures 1,029 square feet and sleeps up to 7.

The Personal Navigator

There is so much to see and do on a daily basis, a passenger could easily become overwhelmed, if not downright

A TENDER SUBJECT

Some ports require a process called "tendering." This means, rather than pulling right up to a dock, the ship will pull close to port and drop anchor. Ferries take guests back and forth to shore. It's an efficient system, but it could knock you for a loop if you're not expecting it—especially if you've got an early excursion booked. In this case, you'll have to leave a whole lot earlier than you originally planned.

discombobulated. Not to worry. An in-house publication called the *Personal Navigator* will help you make the most of every day. Updated daily and delivered to all staterooms, the publication is a comprehensive listing of a day's onboard activities, events, and entertainment.

We simply cannot overemphasize the importance of the daily *Personal Navigator*. It is a truly indispensable tool. When you get your hands on it (the first one should be waiting for you in your stateroom), drop everything and read it cover to cover. In addition to listing the lineup of activities scheduled for the rest of the day (which on day one will include the "Adventures Away" sail away party), it'll provide many other handy bits of information. For instance, in the upper-right corner of the front page, you'll find the suggested evening attire for that day. It changes from day to day, so be sure to note it. It also notes the time and location of Disney character appearances, any points of interest the ship may have scheduled, a notification of any time zone changes, as well as any "special offers" at shops or lounges. Keep an eye out for Internet discounts, too. From this pamphlet, you'll also glean the times of sunrise and sunset, should you aspire to be on an observation deck for Mother Nature's daily presentations.

Dining

A Disney cruise is not the place to count calories— although most special dietary needs can be accommodated upon request. There's no shortage of rations on these ships. If your tastes are simple (say, a hot dog at Pluto's Dog House) or

sublime (how does a juicy filet mignon, courtesy of Palo, sound?), rest assured you'll never be hungry. Or understimulated, for that matter, as many of the restaurants are down-right entertaining. And, thanks to a system called "rotational dining," you'll have a chance to experience three restaurants, all the while being made to feel like a VIP by your serving staff. That means you'll eat at a different one of the three main restaurants each evening, often with the same table guests, and enjoy the services of the same waitstaff. Your serving team gets to know you, as well as your likes and dislikes, very well. The system, which is unique to Disney Cruise Line, tends to get the thumbs-up from cruise veterans and new-comers alike. The only exceptions to the rule are Palo and Remy, the adults-only, reservations-necessary restaurants. (For details on Palo, see page 76; for the *Dream*'s Remy, page 78.)

How do you know where to go on which night? Easy. A ticket with the details will be waiting for you in your stateroom. Don't forget to check the day's *Personal Navigator* to note the style of dress for the evening.

HOT TIP

At table-service restaurants, a gratuity of 15 percent is automatically added to the bill for alcoholic beverages. At bars and lounges, a gratuity is added for all drinks (including soft drinks).

TABLE SERVICE

Each Disney ship has four table-service restaurants, three of which are included in the unique "rotational dining" system. They all serve dinner, but check the *Personal Navigator* for hours and meals served at each spot for the rest of the day.

Animator's Palate

The *pièce de résistance*—as far as Disney creativity goes— is without a doubt Animator's Palate, a place

where diners not only have to decide what to eat, but also what to watch! Simple surprises abound at each stage of the evening meal. This restaurant can be found on all three ships.

Upon entering the all black-and-white dining room, you will be led to your table and asked for your order. Note the soft background music and the black-and-white sketches along the wall. While you're doing so, drinks and appetizers will be served. If you ignore this distraction and keep your gaze fixed on the walls, you may notice a bit of color creeping into

that sketch of Cinderella. By the time the entrées make their entrance, the room is ablaze in living color. The music tends to get a bit livelier by this point, too. You may even notice that your waitstaff becomes more colorful toward meal's end.

The menu has featured items such as salmon wrapped in phyllo dough, beef tenderloin, and other tempting choices. If they're available, we recommend starting with the butternut squash soup and capping it off with a slice of double-fudge chocolate cake. The ice cream is tempting, too.

Enchanted Garden

This picturesque spot, which is located on the *Dream* only, seems truly enchanted, as the immersive, outdoorsy environment transforms from day to night over the course of your meal.

Breakfast, served buffet-style, is offered on select days of each cruise. Ditto for lunch. The daily dinner is a four-course affair of seasonal selections. For an extra charge (plus gratuity), guests may enjoy bar drinks, bottled water, and specialty coffee. Soft drinks (coffee, soda, fruit juice, milk, and tea) carry no charge. This eatery is located on Deck 2, midship on the *Disney Dream*.

Lumière's

Located on the *Magic* only, this elegant spot provides fine dining in a setting inspired by *Beauty and the Beast*. The sprawling dining room is elegant and softly lit, though a bit more raucous than its cosmopolitan contemporaries (see the photo below). Note that the

HOT TIP

If your laptop is equipped for wireless Internet access, bring it along! Several public areas on the Disney ships provide "Wi-Fi" service. On the *Magic*, pay 75 cents a minute or buy a package of 100 minutes for $55, 250 minutes for $100, or 500 minutes for $150. On the *Wonder*, pay $.75 per minute or buy a package of 50 minutes for $27.50, 100 minutes for $40, or 250 minutes for $75. For pricing specifics on the *Dream*, call 800-910-3659.

later seating is usually a tad more sedate.

Menu selections at dinner have included crispy roasted duck breast with braised napa cabbage and aged Angus beef tenderloin. Vegetarians can opt for the porcini mushroom-stuffed pasta in a vegetable broth. And waist-watchers won't feel cheated by the grilled marinated tofu. For

dessert, consider the crème brûlée or soufflé. Sugar-free selections are available, too: chocolate cheesecake and an apple-cinnamon fruit dish served with a fresh-baked brownie.

Triton's

Passengers aboard the *Wonder* may dine in the elegant Triton's, where the

specialty of the house is sea-food. (It is, after all, named for the Little Mermaid's dad, King Triton.) The ocean theme is enhanced by subtly changing lighting with every course, the room getting greener and greener as the meal progresses. Menu items have included French onion soup, three-cheese lobster macaroni, seared sea bass, and braised lamb shank. For dessert, there's chocolate mousse, Grand Marnier soufflé, ice cream sundaes, and more.

Parrot Cay

This tropical spot, which is located on the *Magic* and *Wonder* and is pronounced Parrot *KEY*, is certainly one of the most colorful spaces you'll ever dine in. Done up in vibrant shades of orange, green, blue, and yellow, it boasts a rainbow of cleverly formed napkin displays at each table. The island-like feel has been complemented by such dinner dishes as pan-seared grouper, poached halibut with clams and mussels, Caribbean roasted chicken, and mixed grill. Kids appreciate the macaroni and cheese, a Disney specialty. Dessert-wise, expect the likes of lemon meringue pie with kumquat sauce, chocolate s'more vanilla cake, and French toast banana bread. This place is on the *Magic* and *Wonder* only.

HOT TIP

Beer drinkers take note: If you purchase a refillable mug at the start of the cruise, you will be entitled to discount suds for the duration of your stay aboard the ship. (You must have the mug with you to net the discount.)

Royal Palace

This regal restaurant (on the *Dream* only) got its inspiration from classic Disney animated features such as *Sleeping Beauty*, *Beauty and the Beast*, and *Cinderella*. French-inspired, continental cuisine is offered for breakfast, lunch, and dinner. A buffet is offered on select mornings of each cruise, as is a full-service lunch. A four-course dinner takes place nightly.

Seating Times and Situations

There are normally two seating sessions for dinner; however, the actual times vary depending on what specific itinerary the ship is sailing at the time. The most common times are 5:45 P.M. and 8:15 P.M., and 6 P.M. and 8:30 P.M. If you have a preference, be sure to tell your travel agent or reservationist the moment you book your cruise.

Requests for any seating cannot be guaranteed. If you get closed out of a particular seating time, check with Guest Services after boarding. Sometimes folks switch plans after arrival. Most of the seating at table-service restaurants is communal (with the exception of Palo). If you are traveling as a family with kids, expect to be seated with similar travelers. Adults without kids will be seated together if possible.

Palo

For adults only, Palo is an ideal spot for special celebrations or just a quiet, romantic evening. Offering brunch, dinner, and high tea, Palo's worth the small

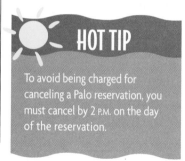

HOT TIP

To avoid being charged for canceling a Palo reservation, you must cancel by 2 P.M. on the day of the reservation.

surcharge (at press time, prices were $15 for brunch and dinner; $5 for high tea) to indulge in a five-star dining experience that includes an ocean view.

True to its roots (*palo* means "pole" in Italian), the restaurant has echoes of Venice, Italy. Masks from that city's *Carnevale* line the walls, and the menu reflects some of the best continental fare you'll find on either side of the Atlantic. For dinner, appetizers include fresh, homemade (and delicious) pizzas and classic Caesar salads with thinly sliced Parmesan cheese. The entrée menu tempts with selections such as lobster and mascarpone ravioli, grilled sea scallops with pancetta, and garlic roasted rack of lamb. A warning: Save room for dessert or you will never forgive yourself. The chocolate soufflé (with hot chocolate and vanilla sauces) is beyond amazing.

HOT TIP

Palo and Remy reservations will not appear on your *Personal Navigator*. (It's not *that* personal!) Make sure you don't miss it. There is an extra per person charge for all meals—show or no-show. Call 800-910-3659 for specifics.

(The soufflé must be ordered in advance.) The pineapple and almond ravioli and Palo's homemade tiramisu yield raves, too.

Brunch at Palo is indeed a special event. (It's offered on cruises of 4 days or more.) The buffet is so vast that it requires a guided tour (which, happily, you will receive). Expect to sample fruit, salads, seafood, pastries, made-to-order omelets, fish, and chicken entrées, and more.

High tea, served at 3:30 P.M. on cruises of seven nights and more, is another way to sample the delights here. A variety of teas is available. Nibbles include finger sandwiches, cookies, cakes, warm scones served with thick cream and jam, as well as other treats.

Palo is for diners ages 18 years and older. Reservations are required and can be made at *www.disneycruise.com,* or at Rockin' Bar D (*Magic*), WaveBands (*Wonder*), or The District (*Dream*) starting at about 1 P.M. on the first day of a cruise. NOTE: *Palo has brunch during 4- and 7-night-or-longer cruises. High tea is offered on 7-night cruises only. Shorts, jeans, bathing suits, and tank tops are not acceptable attire for any meal at Palo.*

Remy

For adults (age 18 and older) on the *Dream*, Remy is a ritzy, palate-pleasing delight. Considered the most upscale dining experience available on the ship, Remy serves fine

HOT TIP

Children's menus are available in all shipboard restaurants (with the obvious exceptions of Palo and Remy). Buffets all stock kid-friendly vittles such as mac and cheese and chicken nuggets.

French-inspired cuisine for dinner. The luxurious dining room features Art Nouveau touches and a rich color scheme. Tables are set with Frette linens, Riedel glassware, Christofle silverware, and custom-created china.

The evening meal begins with a champagne cocktail and continues with 8 to 9 small courses. There's nothing more thrilling than a tableside visit from the trolley of international cheeses—except, perhaps, for the wine decanting stations and after-dinner coffee service.

The private Chef's Table experience takes place in a

special 16-seat dining room and features *Ratatouille*-inspired decor.

Oenophiles appreciate the lovely Wine Room, which accommodates up to 16 guests. Here, guests dine in a glass-walled room with marble flooring amid 900 bottles of wine.

Reservations are required to dine at Remy, and meals served here come with a surcharge. Reservations may be made online (75 days ahead for first-time cruisers, 90 to 120 days ahead for Castaway Club members),

and 120 days in advance for concierge guests.

Like its posh neighbor, Palo, Remy also has a dress code. It is a bit more formal here than at Palo: jackets, dress pants, and dress shoes for men; dresses, suits, blouses, and dress pants for women. (Please leave the jeans, shorts, capri pants, sandals, Crocs, flip-flops, and sneakers in your stateroom.)

What to Wear for Dinner

Generally speaking, "cruise casual" is the way to go in

all spots except for Palo and Remy: collared shirts, blouses, cotton pants, jeans, and sundresses are generally acceptable for evenings in all other restaurants—shorts, swimsuits, T-shirts, and tank tops are not. On select nights, there will be a theme: tropical, pirate attire, semi-formal, etc. On such days, the desired style of dress will be noted in the *Personal Navigator.* (While parents are the best judges of what attire is appropriate for their kids, most guests over the age of 13 are usually comfortable wearing attire that is similar to what is recommended for all passengers.) Note that Palo and Remy, grown-ups-only destinations, are formal and guests are asked to dress accordingly.

Wine and Dine

Each of the table-service restaurants (including Palo and Remy) offers many vintages by the glass or by the bottle. If you order a bottle and fail to finish it by meal's end, ask your server to store it for you. (You will get it with your next evening's meal.)

For guests who expect to enjoy more than one bottle of wine over the course of the cruise, Disney offers two wine packages (both include red and white selections).

Special Dietary Needs

Many special dietary needs, such as low-sodium, low-carb, lactose-free, or kosher meals, may be met aboard Disney cruise ships. All requests should be made well in advance, preferably at the time of booking. It's always a good idea to confirm the request prior to setting sail.

SELF-SERVE, FAST FOOD, AND SNACKS

Vibe

This teen-only spot—found on all ships—offers a selection of (non-alcoholic) smoothie drinks, as well as snacks and other soft drinks. There are lots of games and magazines, and some refreshments are free of charge. However, there is an extra charge for smoothies and specialty drinks. This area is hopping all day—and often past midnight. FYI: The teen-only spots on the *Magic* and *Wonder* used to be Aloft and The Stack, respectively, but were recently renamed Vibe.

HOT TIP

Adults may bring their own (unopened) bottle of wine to dinner. An $18 corking fee will be charged to your shipboard account for each bottle that was not purchased onboard.

FUN FOOD FACTS

Apparently, cruising makes passengers exceptionally hungry. Here's what's put away on an average 7-night voyage on the *Disney Magic*:

- ⚓ Rib-eye steak—800 to 1,000 pounds
- ⚓ Beef strip loin—2,000 pounds
- ⚓ Beef tenderloin—2,500 pounds
- ⚓ Whole chickens—9,000 pounds
- ⚓ Fresh salmon—900 pounds
- ⚓ Grouper—300 pounds
- ⚓ Shrimp—2,200 pounds
- ⚓ Lobster tail—900 pounds
- ⚓ Fresh melon—10,500 pounds
- ⚓ Fresh pineapple—4,400 pounds
- ⚓ Yogurt—2,400 tubs
- ⚓ Cereal—7,920 packets
- ⚓ Individual eggs—44,500
- ⚓ Tomato ketchup—26,000 packets
- ⚓ Mayonnaise—15,000 packets
- ⚓ Sugar—40,000 packets
- ⚓ Beer—7,400 bottles/cans
- ⚓ Wine and champagne—2,200 bottles

Beverage Station

There is a self-serve station on Deck 9 by the Mickey pool. Feel free to help yourself to water, juice, soda, lemonade, iced tea, coffee, hot chocolate, and hot tea. There is an ice machine, too. The station is generally open 24 hours a day, though not all selections are available at all times. (If the machine fails to dispense ice, get room service delivery.) Note that carbonated soft drinks are free here and with meals, but not at bars and lounges or through room service.

Cabanas

Located on the *Dream*, this indoor-outdoor casual eatery serves three meals a day. This spot recalls a breezy boardwalk along the Pacific coast, with a dash of Disney. Made-to-order breakfast and lunch selections are offered "on the boardwalk" on most days (check your *Personal Navigator* for times and specifics). In other words, a variety of food stations proffer freshly prepared edibles. Dinner is a table-service affair. Cocktails may be ordered from the Clam Bar. Cabanas is located on Deck 11, aft.

Cove Cafe

A cozy, adults-only lounge, Cove Cafe can be found aboard all ships. It features espresso and other specialty coffees, and a full bar. Cakes and cookies are available, too. Books and magazines are on hand for on-site perusing, as is a large-screen TV (often showing a big game or the news). Board games may be borrowed, too. Wireless Internet access is available (for a fee). The cafe is near the Quiet Cove Pool.

Pinocchio's Pizzeria

Magic and *Wonder:* A counter-service spot serving spirits and soft drinks (for a fee), and cheese and pepperoni pizzas (no charge for food). There is often a special pizza of the day. Be sure to ask.

Pluto's Dog House

Magic and *Wonder:* Located at the foot of Mickey's Pool, this window serves hot dogs, bratwurst, burgers, veggie burgers, fish burgers, grilled chicken sandwiches, tacos, and chicken tenders.

Goofy's Galley

Magic and *Wonder:* A popular snack spot, this counter specializes in ice cream and frozen yogurt. It also dispenses salads, wraps, panini sandwiches, cookies, and fresh fruit. The selection tends to change throughout the day, so it pays to check back from time to time.

ROOM SERVICE

Stateroom dining service delivers 24 hours a day— very handy if you're traveling with children or if you have a serious snack craving in between meals. Most menu items are included with your cruise package. At press time, selections included soups, salads, sandwiches, burgers, pizza, cookies, and selections for kids. There is a charge for beverages and some snack selections (such as candy, popcorn, wine, beer, soda, and bottled water). Gratuity is not always included.

(Continued on page 86)

BE BORED: WE DARE YOU!

On any given day, guests aboard a Disney ship have a plethora of activities to engage in. On one of our sea days, we were offered the following:

10 A.M. Team Trivia

11 A.M. **Pool Games**

11:30 A.M. Meet Disney Character Friends

1 P.M. **Disney Behind the Scenes** (tour of the Walt Disney Theatre)

1:30 P.M. Character Autograph Session

1:30 P.M. **Family Golf Putting**

2 P.M. "Dive-In" Movie

2 P.M. **Disney's Art of Entertaining** (cake decorating)

2 P.M. Beer Tasting

2:30 P.M. **Wine Tasting**

2:45 P.M. Art of the Theme Show (behind-the-scenes tour)

3 P.M. **Pool Games**

3:30 P.M. Mr. Toad's Wild Race

3:30 P.M. **Jackpot Bingo**

3:30 P.M. High Tea at Palo

4:30 P.M. **Chip It Golf**

4:30–5:30 P.M. Family Basketball Time

4:45–5:30 P.M. **Salsa Dancing**

5:30–6:15 P.M. Dancing Music

5:30 P.M. **Family Sing-Along**

5:45–6:30 P.M. Captain's Welcome Reception

5:45–6:30 P.M. **Family Dance Party**

6:15 P.M. Villains Tonight!

7:30–8:30 P.M. **Family Dance Party**

7:30–8:30 P.M. Pin Trading

7:45–8:30 P.M. **Captain's Welcome Reception**

8:30 P.M. Tailgate Party

8:30 P.M. **Twice Charmed—An Original Twist on the Cinderella Story**

9:30–10:15 P.M. Who Wants to Be a Mouseketeer?

10:15–11:30 P.M. **Family Karaoke**

10:15 P.M. Cabaret Show

10:45 P.M. **Disco Legends Party**

12–2 A.M. Dance Party

Note that some events are repeated to accommodate guests dining early and those with late seatings. Some activities are for grown-ups only. These listings were taken from actual *Personal Navigators*.

(Continued from page 83)

Topsider's Buffet and Beach Blanket Buffet

Located on the *Magic* and *Wonder*, respectively, these self-service buffets offer breakfast and lunch. The morning meal brings selections such as fresh fruit, cereal, eggs, sausage, oatmeal, etc. Lunch fare usually has a theme: Italian, Chinese, seafood, etc. (Check a *Personal Navigator*, or at the eatery itself, to learn if there's a theme for the meal.) In addition to the buffet (which you will encounter as you enter), there is a serving station by the seating area. This area serves omelets in the morning and something special for lunch. There are indoor tables and others out on the deck. Both spots offer table service and casual dining for dinner on most nights.

SPECIAL DINING EXPERIENCES

Pirates IN the Caribbean Party

If there's one thing Disney really knows how to do right, it's throw a party. On one night during every cruise, guests enjoy a buccaneering soirée. If you own any pirate attire or regalia, wear it for the big event. It takes place on the upper decks, where Captain Hook and Mr. Smee set their sights on taking over the ship. An epic battle ensues as the good guys take on the villains. The greatest spectacle of all is the show's grand finale—fireworks (except for the Alaska itinerary). It's the only display of its kind done at sea. A feast fit for a pirate king is served on deck, post pyrotenics.

Character Breakfast

An up-close-and-personal morning starring furry favorites is a very Disney way to start the day. (This is only available on cruises of 7 nights or longer.) Everyone may attend at least one character-hosted breakfast per cruise. Check your Dining Ticket for assigned morning and location (characters vary). Some characters have been known to dance with younger guests. Bring your camera!

Many of the character breakfast selections remain staples—eggs, bacon, cereal, fruit, yogurt, and Mickey French toast, for example.

Till We Meet Again Dinner

Presented on the final evening of cruises 7-nights or longer, this meal is a chance to enjoy new favorite dishes, celebrate new friends, and perhaps start planning (or at least dreaming about) your next cruise. Menu items have included Nori-wrapped salmon and roasted mint-pesto-crusted lamb.

Captain's Gala Dinner

Even on this, one of the planet's most casual of cruises, there is a chance to don your finery and join the sparkle and glitter of this black-tie (optional) affair. If you'd rather not get completely decked out, go with a business casual look (but not too casual). The French-continental menu is offered in each of the main dining rooms on all ships. The Gala is only offered on cruises of 7 nights or longer.

Family Tea

A tea party with one of Disney's beloved characters is a true kid-pleaser. During this break in the day's activities, the party's host will tell stories, sign autographs and pose for pictures. The tea is offered on cruises of 7 nights or longer. Reservations may be made at Guest Services. There is no extra charge.

Bars and Lounges

From elegant spots with live piano music to rousing sports bars, Disney ships have a bounty of bars and lounges in which to wet your whistle or simply unwind and watch the waves or the sunset. Note that most drinks offered in these spots come with an extra charge.

Bon Voyage

A casual lounge located on Deck 3, midship (*Dream*). Beverages and snacks are available all day.

Cadillac Lounge

Unique to the Route 66 entertainment zone (*Wonder*), this sophisticated spot celebrates classic cars and soothing music.

Cove Cafe

A cozy adults-only lounge, Cove Cafe can be found aboard all three Disney ships. It offers espresso, specialty coffees, and a full bar. Snacks are available, too. Books and magazines are on hand for on-site perusing, as is a large-screen TV. Board games may also be borrowed for on-site use. Wireless Internet is available (for a fee).

Currents

A breezy spot with stellar ocean views, Currents can be found on Deck 13, forward (*Dream*).

District Lounge

This intimate bar is located in the *Dream*'s District entertainment zone.

Evolution Lounge

A butterfly-themed hotspot, Evolution celebrates all styles of music. Located in the *Dream*'s District area, this space hosts family activities by day and dance parties by night—plus karaoke. (Guests must be at least 18 to come here at night, 21 to imbibe.)

Meridian Bar
A *Dream* exclusive, Meridian is located on Deck 12, aft next to Palo, and has both indoor and outdoor seating.

Outlook Bar
Overlooking the Quiet Cove Pool on the *Magic* and *Wonder* (grown-ups only), this bar serves cocktails and soft drinks.

Pink
An elegant nightspot designed to look like the inside of a Champagne bottle, this lounge is in the *Dream*'s District entertainment zone.

Promenade Lounge
This lounge serves drinks throughout the day on the *Magic* and *Wonder*. At night, it offers live music.

Rockin' Bar D
This Beat Street joint (*Magic*) fancies itself a roadhouse honky-tonk. Expect to hear lots of deejay-selected tunes. There's a dance floor, plus tables and bar seating. Themed parties are thrown here on select nights.

Sessions
The *Magic*'s version of an intimate piano bar, this elegant lounge serves cocktails and caviar.

Signals
Located on Deck 9 of the *Magic*, this poolside spot serves spirits (including the daily special) and soft drinks.

Skyline

The *Dream*'s District area is home to Skyline, a cosmopolitan bar with majestic views of famous cities from around the world.

Sports Bar

A sports fan's dream come true, this lounge has a satellite feed (often showing more than one game at a time), plus suds and (occasionally) wings, hot dogs, and other munchies. It's called Diversions on the *Magic* and *Wonder* and Metro Pub on the *Dream*.

Vista Café

Grown-up *Dream* guests in need of a java jolt can head to this cheery destination on Deck 4, midship. Snacks and cocktails are served, too.

WaveBands

Vintage radios and album covers line the walls and set the stage for a lively dance club. A deejay keeps the place grooving till the wee hours. All manner of drinks are available at this Route 66 club (*Wonder*).

Waves

Overlooking the *Dream*'s Mickey's Pool, this casual spot serves beverages throughout the day.

Entertainment

For some, a deck chair, a good book, and a steady stream of sunshine is all the entertainment required. Others may delight in an evening of dancing or a bingo-filled afternoon. And some are satisfied with nothing short of an all-out Broadway-style musical stage show. Fortunately, Disney Cruise Line has all of the above, plus guest lecturers, behind-the-scenes tours, and a whole lot more. Check the daily *Personal Navigator* for show schedules. Note that all shows are not presented every day. And keep in mind that the entertainment lineup is tweaked from time to time, so some details may differ during your cruise.

STAGE SHOWS

The majestic Walt Disney Theatre (Deck 4, forward) is the venue in which Disney Cruise Line presents a lineup of lavish Broadway-style musical performances. Among them: *Toy Story—The Musical*; *Disney Dreams—An Enchanted Classic*; *Twice Charmed—An Original Twist on the Cinderella Story*; *The Golden Mickeys*; and *Villains Tonight!*

The vast auditorium, which spans several decks, also hosts variety shows, the big-payoff final bingo game, and more.

The Golden Mickeys

A dynamic production that pays tribute to the musical legacy of Walt Disney Studios. It's got all the glitz and glamour of a Hollywood celebration, paying homage to the comedy, romance, and heroes (plus a few key villains) of classic Disney animated films. This show is presented on the *Wonder*. It's a big crowd-pleaser (and worthy of a Golden Mickey)!

All Aboard: Let the Magic Begin

This sweet presentation is a terrific way to "meet" your ship's crew. The captain, cruise director, and many of their comrades introduce themselves and

DID YOU KNOW?

The anchor on the *Disney Magic* weighs 28,200 pounds—about the same as three full-grown elephants!

welcome everyone aboard. Musical numbers and vaudeville-like variety acts round out the bill. This show is a *Disney Magic* exclusive.

Disney Dreams—An Enchanted Classic

This bedtime story features a galaxy of characters, including Peter Pan, Belle, Beast, Aladdin, Cinderella, and Ariel. Together and through the power of song (and dance), the characters teach a skeptical girl about the power of dreams. It takes place on all ships.

Toy Story—The Musical

Fans of the beloved movie will be pleased to see it come to life in one of the largest productions ever developed for a cruise ship. The story isn't entirely new—but the music is. The tunes help tell the story of Buzz, Woody, and the gang of toys from Andy's room in an ambitious way. This show is presented exclusively on the *Wonder*.

Twice Charmed—An Original Twist on the Cinderella Story

A Broadway-style extravaganza (*Magic* only), this musical production begins with the wedding of Cinderella and Prince Charming. Things take a sudden turn when the wicked Fairy Godfather makes his presence known and, after granting a wish to one evil stepmother, sends the family back in time, where—*gasp*—the glass slipper gets broken! Does this turn of events destroy Cinderella's chances of living happily ever after? You'll have to catch the show to find out.

Remember the Magic: A Final Farewell

This show wraps up the trip as performers celebrate a week of shipboard activities and island-hopping. *Disney Magic* only.

DECK PARTIES

When it comes to on-deck celebrations, the area by the family pool (Goofy's or Mickey's, depending on the ship) is party central. Starting with the festive "Adventures Away" Sail Away Celebration and continuing with daily dance fests with Disney characters, live bands, and fireworks (except for Alaska itineraries), it seems like there is always a reason to party. Check the daily *Personal Navigator* for celebration specifics.

FAMILY ENTERTAINMENT

D Lounge

This family-friendly lounge and nightclub is located on the *Dream* (Deck 4, midship).

Studio Sea

A colorful "TV studio" environment is the setting for audience-participation family game shows. *Mickey Mania* lets you put your knowledge of Disney trivia to the test, while *Karaoke Night* encourages families to take the stage and sing together. Finally, the *Family Dance Party* gives everyone a chance to kick up their heels (or sneakers) and enjoy a party for guests of all ages. Keep in mind that the entertainment lineup, though always dynamic, is subject to change.

Character Breakfast

On all cruises that are seven nights or longer, a breakfast is hosted by Disney friends.

HOT TIP

Looking for a little privacy on the *Magic* or *Wonder*? There is a little-known outdoor nook—complete with comfy chairs—on Deck 7, aft.

Family Tea

Guests of all ages, but especially little ones (on 7-night cruises or longer), are invited to enjoy afternoon tea with Wendy Darling or Alice and the Mad Hatter at Studio Sea. In addition to learning the proper way to serve tea and cookies, guests are treated to stories about their hostess's adventures. Tickets are necessary and are available at Guest Services (they're free). For details on afternoon tea, turn to page 87.

FOR GROWN-UPS ONLY

The over-18 set on the *Magic* and *Wonder* can attend intriguing demonstrations (i.e., Disney's Art of Entertaining), lectures and conversations with guest speakers, tours (of the ship's galley and other areas of interest), specially tailored nighttime events (such as *Match Your Mate*, a game show in which you and your mate will find out how much you know about each other), as well as theme nights, cabaret shows, and more.

JUST FOR KIDS

The kids' programs and activities tend to elicit raves from participants and parents alike. For starters, adults who leave their kids at supervised facilities can be assured that the watchword here is safety. There are 47 counselors, with a ratio of one counselor for every six children in the toddler age group, one for every 15 kids in the age 3-to-4 demographic, and one for every 25 in the 5-to-12 crowd. The secured programming allows counselors to know where every child is at any given time (kids are checked in with Youth Activities when entering and signed out when exiting with an authorized guardian).

Records of a child's allergies or other particular needs are entered into their file.

Every youngster is required to wear a wristband that identifies him or her as a participant in the program. Parents get beepers and can be contacted immediately if their child has a problem or just wants to see them.

Cleanliness is a priority, too. In fact, kids entering the Oceaneer Club and Lab are promptly asked to put out their hands. After a quick squirt of liquid soap, they wash up before engaging in any of the activities. Play areas are cleaned three times a day, with a deep-down cleansing done at the end of each day.

The children's programs are divided up here. They are concentrated on Deck 5, but supervised groups may leave the designated play areas. The specially tailored programming is open to kids who are completely potty-trained, able to interact comfortably within the counselor-to-child ratio groups, and able to mix well with peers.

A child may participate in an older age group if he or she is within one month of the minimum age for that group. If your kids simply can't bear to be separated, know that older kids may stay with their younger siblings.

Kids who exhibit symptoms of illness—even if it's just a runny nose—will not be allowed to participate. If a child becomes disruptive, he or

she may not be allowed to participate without a parent or guardian present.

Except for the nursery, there is no fee to participate in youth activities. The following descriptions of the youth activities were accurate at press time, but specifics are subject to change from time to time.

Oceaneer Club

A wonderfully detailed adventure zone, this club has several distinctly themed areas on the *Dream* and a pirate theme on the *Magic* and *Wonder*. In addition to computer games, costumes, and other games, there are many organized activities. It's open to kids ages 3–10 on the *Magic* and *Dream*, and 3–12 on the *Wonder*.

Among the activities for the 3- and 4-year-olds are: *Mouseketeer Training* (where children train to be Mouse-keteers (the Mouse himself pops in to inspect the new crew of recruits and even leads them in a march), *Magical Adventures with Wendy* (an adventure with music, games, and the story of Neverland, with Wendy Darling), and *Do-Si-Do with Snow White* (dancing with one of the Enchanted Forest's most famous residents).

Kids enjoy activities such as *So You Want to Be a Pirate?* (where a very theatrical swashbuckler—a buddy of Captain Hook—tells tales of buccaneer adventures), *Toy Story Boot Camp* (where a green army man leads "recruits" in a series of activities and craft projects), *Stitch's Great Adventure* (a program that invites youngsters to help

Stitch capture ten of his lost "experiments"), and *Flubber* (where kids join a wacky professor to explore a squishy green mystery substance). Lunch and dinner are served.

Oceaneer Lab

The Lab is open to kids (ages 3–12 on the *Wonder*, and ages 3–10 on the *Magic* and *Dream*), with the kids on the *Wonder* divided into groups made up of 8- and 9-year-olds and another with those ages 10–12. The room is filled with wacky inventions and opportunities for exploration. There are music stations, games, computers, video games, drawing materials, and more. As with the Oceaneer Club, there are also several imaginative organized activities.

Kids ages 8–9 can enjoy programs such as *Flubber* (and in doing so encounter solid liquids and mix a batch of green goop), *Animation Antics* (which unlocks some of the secrets of Disney animation), and *Ratatouille Cooking School* (which lets kids help bake cookies).

Kids in the 10–12 group experience *Flubber* (where kids gain insight into the magic of science), *All For One: High School Musical Mad Cap Caper* (inspired by the trio of wildly popular H.S.M. movies), *Ship Factor*

HOT TIP

When the weather's good, it's breezy on deck. When the weather's less than perfect, it is breezier. When the weather's bad, it's downright gusty. If you've got long hair and you intend to explore outside deck areas, bring a band or a clip to tie your hair back.

(which challenges teams in bizarre and wacky competitions), and more. Lunch and dinner are served.

Reminder: *Kids ages 8–12 may check themselves in and out of the Oceaneer Lab with their parents' permission.*

Ocean Quest

On the *Magic,* kids ages 11–13 can play Captain as they steer the ship from this scaled replica of the bridge. LCD screens let kids get a simulated view from the *Magic*'s bridge. There are video games, arts and crafts, and plasma-screen TVs for movie-viewing as well. There are space-themed evening activities such as scavenger hunts and karaoke parties, too. Ocean Quest is unique to the *Magic.*

Edge

A tweens-exclusive space, Edge is located on Deck 13 inside the forward funnel aboard the *Dream.*

Flounder's Reef Nursery and Small World Nursery

Open to children ages 12 weeks through 3 years, these colorful spaces are the ships' babysitting centers. (Flounder's Reef can be found on the *Magic* and *Wonder*, while Small World is the name of the nursery on the *Dream.*) For an hourly fee the nursery offers toddler-friendly activities and a quiet area, complete with cribs.

No food is available at the nursery, but if parents provide prepared bottles or jarred food that is clearly labeled with a child's name, staffers will happily feed their hungry tyke. Space is limited and gets booked early. In fact, reservations are accepted via *www. disneycruise.com* and on embarkation day on a first-come, first-served basis. Due to the high demand, multiple requests may not be honored—so don't count on securing several sessions, though it can't hurt to try. The fee for the babysitting service is $6 per hour for the first child, $5 per each additional child with a one-hour minimum (siblings net the discount). *In-stateroom babysitting is not available on any ship.*

TEENS ONLY

Teens can enjoy their own special hangouts and activities while aboard Disney ships. Vibe is their exclusive place to hang out (If you're old enough to vote, KEEP OUT!). It's got popular music, games, dance parties, big-screen TVs, Internet access (for a fee), snacks, and more. The activities and sodas are free, but smoothies cost extra. Other teen-oriented programs include karaoke, organized sports activities, a pool party, and more.

NOW IT'S TIME...

...to say good-bye. At the end of the cruise, kids who participated in children's programs can take part in a good-bye celebration called Friendship Rocks! Presented at the Walt Disney Theatre, the musical celebration is quite popular—even Mickey and Minnie join in the festivities—so arrive early for a good seat. Note that all pint-sized participants receive a souvenir T-shirt to mark the occasion.

FUN AND GAMES
Arcade

Located on Deck 9 on the *Magic* and *Wonder* by Goofy's Family Pool, Quarter Master's Arcade is a small room replete with modern electronic games and an air hockey table. On the *Dream*, the pirate-themed—and appropriately named—Arr-cade can be found on Deck 11. You will have to purchase credits to play in any of the ships' arcades.

Bingo

Perhaps it's something in the ocean air, but nothing brings out the bingo fanatic in you like a few days at sea. The closest thing to gambling that you'll find on a Disney vessel, the daily bingo tournaments are extremely popular. You have to be at least 18 to play, but kids can watch over Mom or Dad's shoulder and cheer them on. Each session has several individual games. Boards can be purchased one at a time or in bunches. Beware the hard-sell push to get the "grand plan." It's nearly impossible to keep track of all those boards. There is a rolling jackpot—meaning that if no one wins the big prize one day, it rolls over to the next session. That is until the last day bingo is played. Then they call numbers until somebody wins. (On a recent cruise, a lucky guest won a $7,000 jackpot. Sadly, it wasn't us.) *Warning*: The banter of the bingo callers can become a tad cloying. Whatever you do, don't encourage them.

Games

Ping-pong, foosball, shuffleboard, basketball . . . they're all here. Equipment can usually be found by the tables or courts. (Don't monopolize it—it's for everyone to share.) Borrow games from Guest Services. Kooky competitions are sometimes held poolside. See a *Personal Navigator* for details.

Movies

The Buena Vista Theatre shows new film releases—some in dazzling 3-D (courtesy of Disney's patented technology). This is the perfect place to head when the weather is less than ideal. Get there early, as the 268 seats fill up quickly. It is located on Deck 5, aft.

If you prefer your flicks alfresco, make a beeline for the Goofy or Donald pool. A jumbo screen (affixed to the forward funnel and appropriately known as Funnel Vision) broadcasts Disney features, popular television shows, and sporting events at various times throughout the cruise.

SHOPPING

While onboard Disney's cruise ships, you can enjoy tax-free (on all items) and duty-free (select items) shopping. Check the *Personal Navigator* for hours and details about special merchandise events such as pin-trading or Captain's Signing (when the captain autographs collectibles that can be purchased onboard).

DISNEY CRUISE LINE GIFTS

Whether you'll be celebrating a special occasion or simply consider the cruise a special occasion unto itself, you may want to have a gift item delivered to your stateroom as an added surprise. Among the items than can be pre-ordered by visiting *disneycruise.com* are flower arrangements, food and beverage packages, wine selections, and Disney Cruise Line merchandise. Once onboard, you can order via stateroom phone. Allow at least 24 hours for delivery.

The shops have limited hours due to U.S. Customs regulations and can't operate during any time when the ship is in port. Use your stateroom key (Key to the World) to buy items in the ship's shops and on Castaway Cay. (The island's post office accepts cash only.)

(Continued on page 103)

DUTY-FREE SHOPPING—RULES TO SHOP BY

If unlimited duty-free shopping sounds too good to be true, well, it is. There are limits. Federally enforced limits. Specifics vary slightly, depending on where you do your shopping. Know that the rules are mandated by U.S. law and are subject to change.

⚓ **Bahamas**—Each guest re-entering the U.S. from the Bahamas can bring up to $800 (U.S. currency) worth of duty-free treasures. Those of legal drinking age (that's 21 and up) can pick up two liters of alcohol, of which one must be produced in the Bahamas. Legal adults (that's the 18-and-over crowd) are limited to 200 cigarettes and 100 cigars (with the exception of Cuban cigars—they're illegal to bring to the U.S.).

⚓ **Eastern Caribbean**—Guests who voyage to the Eastern Caribbean and back to the U.S. can bring back up to $1,600 worth of duty-free stuff. However, no more than $800 of it can be purchased on the ship, St. Maarten, and Castaway Cay combined. The rest has to come from St. Thomas. Or, the entire $1,600 may be used toward purchases made on St. Thomas alone. Got that? If not, read it again—it's important. As for alcohol, each legal drinker is limited to five liters—only one liter can come from St. Maarten or the ship, with an additional four liters being exempt if they were purchased on St. Thomas and at least one liter of that allotment was produced in the U.S. Virgin Islands. Each guest 18 or older is limited to five cartons of cigarettes (only one carton may be purchased on St. Maarten or the ship, with an additional four cartons being exempt if purchased on St. Thomas). You're allowed 100 cigars (no Cubans).

⚓ **Western Caribbean**—If you are returning from the Western Caribbean to the U.S., you may bring up to $800 worth of duty-free booty from Grand Cayman, Cozumel, and Castaway Cay. If you're at least 21 years old, you can buy one liter of alcohol. Older than 18? You're entitled to 200 cigarettes and 100 cigars (again, don't even *think* of bringing in Cuban cigars).

(Continued from page 101)

ONBOARD SHOPS

Preludes
(Magic and Wonder)

There is a well-stocked snack bar-concession window on either side of the Walt Disney Theatre. It usually closes at about 10 P.M., but opens at different times. Among the items for sale are cookies, candies, nuts, lollipops, and drinks (spirits and soft drinks are served).

Mickey's Mates
(Magic and Wonder)

Located on Deck 4, forward, this retail spot offers Disney Cruise Line logo merchandise, including souvenirs, clothing, beach towels, swimwear, character costumes, gifts, postcards, mugs, and plush toys.

Treasure Ketch
(Magic and Wonder)

Directly across the hall from Mickey's Mates on Deck 4, this shop sells jewelry, loose gemstones, and limited-edition Disney collectibles. There's a selection of clothing, including shirts, sweatshirts, hats, jackets, and other Disney Cruise Line logo items. Duty-free fragrances are available, too. The store also stocks batteries, postcards, disposable cameras, books, magazines, sun-care products, and a limited selection of sundries (including Dramamine). Be sure to check out the nightly promotions—there is a new one each day.

Up Beat and Radar Trap
(Magic and Wonder)

Located on Deck 3, forward, these counter-service spots offer tax- and duty-free liquor, snacks, and more. Note that any liquor purchased here may not be consumed while onboard. It will be delivered to your room on the last evening of your cruise. Everything else may be consumed (or worn) during the cruise.

SHOPS ON CASTAWAY CAY
Buy the Seashore
This new shop offers island-themed souvenirs such as hats, totes, and shirts, plus beach toys, towels, and drinkware. Also available are sun-care products and camera supplies.

Castaway Cay Post Office
They keep things simple here: stamps only. We recommend purchasing stamps at the beginning of the day. Cash only, please.

She Sells Seashells and Everything Else
Have to have a Castaway Cay hat, pin, or T-shirt? This is the place to get it. A mini-bazaar comprised of a hut or two and outdoor stands, "She" also sells beach toys, towels, batteries, sun-care products, tropical wear for the whole family, and, of course, collectible pins and Disney character toys. You'll also find postcards, beach attire, and more.

SPORTS AND RECREATION
Health Club
A state-of-the-art work-out room, the health club is located within the Vista Spa & Salon on the *Magic* and *Wonder* and within the Senses Spa & Salon on the *Dream*. There is no fee to use the health club equipment, which includes treadmills, bikes, stair-

climbing machines, a huge selection of weights, and more. (Some of the gym equipment sport their own TVs—bring headphones or borrow a pair at the front desk.) One-on-one fitness consultations are offered. The health club, as well as the rest of the spa areas, is reserved for adults. The fitness center is generally open from about 6 A.M. to 10 P.M., while the spa is usually open from 8 A.M. to 8 P.M.

Wide World of Sports Deck
(Magic and Wonder)

Deck 10 is home to the Wide World of Sports deck. Though open to everyone, it's a huge kid and teen magnet. The basketball hoops are hopping day and night. Basketballs and other equipment are on-site (no charge). This deck is also popular with casual strollers, though jogging on

GAME ON!

Heads up, sports fans. There is a dedicated sports pub on each of the Disney cruise ships. The laid-back location is called Diversions on the *Magic* and *Wonder* and Metro Pub on the *Dream*. It's a sprawling, TV-filled room with a multitude of live events being broadcast at any time. There's often a mini-buffet available (think wings or hot dogs) and plenty of suds to wash down the snacks. (Snacks are free, but all beverages are extra.) If there's a particular game you're interested in, ask about it at the door. This spot is ideal for watching football, with up to six games shown at a time. Baseball is also a popular draw, as is pro basketball. The occasional hockey match-up is shown, too. We love it here!

the *Magic* and *Wonder* is relegated to Deck 4 (where one lap is equal to about one-third of a mile). Deck 4 is where you'll find the shuffle board court, too.

Goofy's Sports Deck
(Dream)

Located on Deck 13, aft, the always bustling Goofy's Sports Deck is an all-ages, open-air activity center. The basketball court is easily converted to a volleyball court or a small soccer arena. Goofy's deck also boasts virtual sports simulators (soccer, golf, tennis, and basketball), and an honest-to-goodness (or is that Goof-ness?) mini golf course (designed by Goofy and his son, Max).

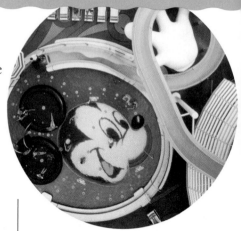

Speaking of Max, he has created two mini courts for little ones to play soccer, basketball, and more.

A walking/jogging track encircles the sports deck, which also features ping-pong and foosball.

Swimming
(Magic and Wonder)

There are three guest swimming pools onboard, all located on Deck 9: Mickey's Pool (for kids) is located toward the back, or aft. Goofy's Family Pool is midship. And the Quiet Cove Adult Pool is on Deck 9, forward. Though the names are self-explanatory, we'll state the obvious: Mickey's pool is for the young'uns and their friends. The Quiet Cove pool is earmarked strictly for splashers ages 18 and up. Don't let the name fool you; Quiet Cove may be for grown-ups, but it isn't always the picture of serenity. Organized games engage giddy adults from time to time. Finally, Goofy's pool is for everyone, but kids under age 10 must be accompanied by an adult, and all swimmers must be potty-trained. Goofy's pool and Quiet Cove have two whirlpools each. Mickey's pool, which, incidentally, is in the shape of the Big Cheese's head, has a special element: Mickey's Splash Zone. The soft-surface spray area is reserved for non-potty-trained tots.

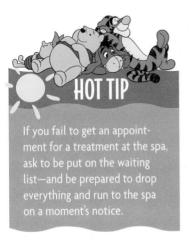

HOT TIP

If you fail to get an appointment for a treatment at the spa, ask to be put on the waiting list—and be prepared to drop everything and run to the spa on a moment's notice.

Babies *must* wear swim diapers at all times.

Swimming
(Dream)

Deck 11 is pool central on this ship. Donald's Pool is the family pool and can be found mid-ship. Mickey's Pool is strictly for kids and their guardians, and the Quiet Cove pool is a grown-ups-only splash zone. Nemo's Reef is a soft-surface spray zone for the toddler set (water-proof diapers are required).

Tired of all that poolside relaxation? Head for Deck 12 and the ship's ultimate adrenaline-inducer: The AquaDuck. This 765-foot-long "water coaster" propels guests through a clear tube on a thrilling journey that includes a trip over the ocean and through the forward funnel, and a four-deck drop into a lazy river. Check your *Personal Navigator* for AquaDuck operating hours.

Spa & Salon
(All ships)

Pampering, Disney style, can be enjoyed at the ships' respective ocean-view spas and salons—Vista Spa & Salon on the *Magic* and *Wonder* and Senses Spa & Salon on the *Dream*. Here, fitness-minded folk can work with a trainer and get instruction in aerobics, or work out in the fitness center. As for the pampering, well, that can come by way of any number of treatments.

Book appointments ahead of time by visiting *www.disneycruise.com*, or go directly to the spa when you first board the ship.

Reservations aren't taken until 1 P.M., but the line forms fast. The Spa & Salon is open to guests ages 18 and older.

The spa is open from 8 A.M. to 8 P.M. every day, *except* on days when the ship is docked at its home port. Prices are posted in the spa. If you miss a reserved treatment, your stateroom will be charged. Note that Cabana Massages (on Castaway Cay) and the Vista Spa villas (luxurious, indoor-outdoor treatment villas [available for one or two] at Vista Spa) are booked here, too. Here's a sampling of treatments:

HAIRDRESSING AND NAIL SERVICES

The salons offer hair styling, plus manicures and pedicures (including a milk-nourishing ritual for the hands and a peppermint ritual for the feet).

WELL-BEING MASSAGE

This 50-minute treatment indulges the whole body and was inspired by cultural touches from around the world. Cost is about $118.

ELEMIS AROMA SPA OCEAN WRAP WITH HALF-BODY MASSAGE

The goal of this treatment is to help restore balance and harmony. Stress is eased away with a combination of aromatherapy, a seaweed mask, and a blend of essential oils that is applied to your body before you are cocooned in a warm wrap. This is followed by a half-body massage. The treatment lasts about 75 minutes. Cost is $188.

LA THERAPIE HYDRALIFT FACIAL

A "youth-enhancing" facial that promises fast and dramatic results. The appearance of fine lines and wrinkles is reduced, skin tone and texture are restored, and the complexion becomes smoother. The 50-minute treatment costs $115.

TROPICAL RAIN FOREST

Experience the benefits of steam, heat, and water therapy combined with the power of aromatherapy to relax the mind and body. Pair it with a treatment and a visit costs just $8. A one-day pass is $15. Unlimited cruise passes are available, too (prices vary).

PORTS OF CALL

To many travelers, the mere experience of being onboard a ship is reward enough; to others, the destinations are the reason to sail. To us, it's a bit of each—so be it faraway places with strange-sounding names or luxurious beach resorts, these ports of call offer something for everyone.

We have made every effort to experience all of the "port adventures" that are detailed in this chapter, but new ones are always possible. For the scoop on the latest additions to the port and excursion lineup and, especially, for ports on the West Coast and Mediterranean itineraries, visit *www.disneycruise.com*. That said, know that none of the port adventures are run by Disney Cruise Line—not even those on Castaway Cay. While Disney strives to oversee the manner in which they are operated, levels of excellence vary. On the pages that follow, you'll find an overview of each Caribbean and Bahamian port and brief descriptions of many tours and adventures that are offered, followed by personal experiences. Remember, you have the freedom to wander about and experience all ports of call at your leisure. This chapter is just intended to provide guidance should you be interested in signing up for "organized" fun.

Be aware that the tours described here may change without notice; we hope the general descriptions and personal views will aid you in your selection. Enjoy.

COZUMEL

Welcome to the biggest island in Mexico! The 28-mile-long island, which gets its name from the Mayan phrase *cuzam huzil*, meaning "land of the swallows," is in the Caribbean, just 12 miles off the mainland. Home to the Palancar Reef (the second-largest diving reef in the world), it's no wonder that Cozumel is a magnet for underwater explorers and snorkelers.

Legend and lore abound here. Centuries ago, in about 300 A.D., the island was a shrine to Ixchel, the goddess of the moon and fertility. (It is said that, when angered, she vents her wrath through violent hurricanes and torrential rains. So don't make her angry . . .)

The area is still rich in ancient sites. Here you will discover the history of a centuries-old culture in its ruins and churches—echoes of the past just waiting for modern-day explorers.

Cozumel is a scuba diver's paradise (it was a favorite destination of the late undersea explorer Jacques Cousteau). Its splendid coral reefs and tropical fish make it irresistible to divers, and fishing aficionados won't be disappointed either: The island's 600-feet-deep waters are populated by marlin, grouper, mackerel, and sailfish—in fact, several world sailfish records have been set here. Actually, it's a place for everyone—even golfers can satisfy an urge here. Intrigued? Read on.

SNORKELING ALERT

Snorkeling excursions are offered at most of the ports frequented by Disney Cruise Line. Olympic swimming skills aren't necessary, as all snorkelers are required to wear a snorkel vest, but guests should be comfortable in the water. Some tips:

- Before jumping in, ask the guide how much time you have and what signal to look for when it's time to return to the boat.

- The mask strap should rest above the ears (or it'll slip down the face).

- Keep hair out of the mask.

- If you can't see anything without your glasses, consider getting a prescription swimmer's mask before you leave home.

- If the mask fogs up, spit inside it. Rub the saliva around, dip it in the ocean water, and replace the mask.

- If water gets in the breathing tube, blow hard through the tube or remove the mouthpiece and empty.

- Bring an underwater camera—and wrap the strap around your wrist.

- Listen to your guide: He or she will alert you to any potential danger.

- There is a first-aid kit on the boat for minor cuts and scrapes.

- Bring a towel from the Disney ship. You'll need it. (Don't forget to bring it back!)

Jeep Exploration
(4.5 hours; Ages 8 and up)

Buckle up and prepare for a memorable—if very bumpy—journey of discovery on this guided Jeep tour into ancient Mexico. After the tour, there's time to hit the beach (a Mexican-style lunch is provided). Jeeps accommodate groups of four. The driving is shared among guests, so be sure to bring your driver's license—and be aware that it's a stick shift here (as in, no automatic transmission).

Unless you are an experienced (and we do mean experienced) driver, skip this one. To describe the terrain as bumpy is an understatement. The beach is nice, but not necessarily worth the grueling ride.

⚓ Adults: $85 (ages 10 and above)
   Children: $75 (ages 8–9)

Mayan Frontier Horseback Riding Tour
(4 hours; Ages 12 and up)

You'll really think you've traveled back in time (way back to about 2000 B.C.) when you hop on a horse and see replicas of ruins along the Mayan frontier, a tropical savanna with echoes of another era. Visit a working ranch stocked with cattle, ponies, and other requisite ranch critters. When you're done, soft drinks and beer await you before you return to the ship—and the 21st century.

What We Think

Equestrians were pleased with this one. It was well run and good for riders of all ages. It is most enjoyable when the temperature is on the less-than-steamy side.

⚓ Adults: $89 (ages 12–65)
   Maximum weight: 240 lbs.

115

Fury Catamaran Sail, Snorkel, and Beach Party
(4.5–5 hours; Ages 5 and up)

Enjoy the best of all possible worlds on this outing. Your magic carpet is a luxurious 65-foot catamaran replete with sundeck and shady areas. The day includes a snorkeling adventure (all equipment provided) and a beach party complete with kayaks and volleyball. If that's not enough, complimentary soft drinks are yours for the asking, as are margaritas and beer (as long as you're at least 21 years old).

 Adventurous types, especially teens, love this one. After the snorkeling, the party really gets underway—and the grown-ups find the margaritas marvelous.

⚓ Adults: $58 (ages 10 and above)
   Children: $31 (ages 5–9)

Mexican Cuisine Workshop & Tasting
(5–5.5 hours; Ages 14 and up)

You're in Mexico. What better place to get a crash course in Mexican cuisine? After a 25-minute ride to Playa Mia Grand Beach Park, an expert chef shares "scrumptious secrets" and guides guests as they prepare a full-course feast. Folks who've already celebrated their 21st birthday may enjoy the open bar while they cook. Following the two-hour food fiesta, there's time to swim or relax on the beach before heading back to the ship. Note that all participants must be able to stand for at least one hour.

 It's a nice alternative to the more active, water-oriented excursions. Yet, standing for more than an hour isn't for everyone.

⚓ Adults: $79 (ages 14 and above)

Tulum Ruins
(7–7.5 hours; Ages 5 and up)

Imagine leaving your cruise ship and (after a 45-minute ferry ride) boarding a bus to the past. That's what you'll do on this archaeological tour. The sacred Mayan city of Tulum is the destination, a knowledgeable guide is your invaluable companion, and the remnants of a fascinating civilization are yours to explore. There's short time to enjoy the nearby beach, and soft drinks and sandwiches are included in the price of the tour. A few notes: There is an additional charge to use *your own* video camera. Since the terrain is not stroller friendly (read: *not allowed*) and requires a lot of walking, this tour is not recommended for children under age 8.

While fascinating, this is a very long day. Our guide was informative, but our hardy crew agreed that this is best left to the archaeological-minded traveler. Kids may get restless—there's a lot of travel time.

⚓ Adults: $99 (ages 10 and above)
Children: $75 (ages 5–9)

Xcaret Eco Archaeological Park

(7–7.5 hours; All ages)

There's so much to see here that the powers that be have decided to leave you on your own to explore. Snorkel (equipment is *not* included, but is available to rent), soak up some culture at the museum, visit the aquarium and bird sanctuary, stop at the stables, delight in the blooms at the botanical gardens, explore the ancient ruins. It's all here. Did we mention the beautiful beaches? Or the lunch and transportation to the park? Enough said.

 Many folks agree that this is a good way to take in a little bit of everything in a lot of hours. Young children got cranky by the end of the day, but overall the reports were positive.

⚓ Adults: $105 (ages 10 and above)
  Children: $80 (ages 9 and under)

Dune Buggy & Beach Snorkel Combo

(4–4.5 hours; Ages 8 and up)

Guests board a customized dune buggy—a four-seater convertible—for a quick trip to a 60-minute snorkel experience. After bonding with fish, it's back to the buggy for a scenic (if lengthy) drive to the beach. Expect to enjoy about an hour at the ocean's edge. A Mexican snack buffet is provided. There are shopping opportunities, so you may want to bring along some cash.

 Dune buggies rock! And you might even get to drive— provided that you're 18 years old and have a valid driver's license. Of course, we're always up for snorkeling and sun worshipping, but could do without the long commute.

⚓ Adults: $92 (ages 10 and above)
  Children: $80 (ages 8–9)

Cozumel Beach Break
(4.5–5 hours; All ages)

Playa Mia is a place for splashing in the pool, lying on the sand, and prancing at the playground. It's all here and all yours for a four-hour respite from—well, from all your other cruising respites. Included in the fee is admission to the pool and use of beach facilities, water toys, and other games. There is an open bar serving mixed drinks, beer, soda, and juice, and a buffet lunch is provided. The beach is accessible via taxi from the pier. There's an additional charge for motorized water sports.

 A nice outing. We always enjoy a day at the beach.

⚓ Adults: $66 (ages 10 and above)
Children: $49 (ages 3–9)
Under age 3: free

Speed Boat Beach Escape
(4 hours; Ages 10 and up)

Barracuda Beach is the place where you can take the wheel of a two-person speed boat (maximum speed: 20 mph) and go on an hour-long tour of the turquoise waters of the Caribbean. Afterward, consider relaxing or playing some volleyball back on Barracuda Beach. A light buffet and beverages are provided. Guests must be at least 18 and be a bearer of a valid driver's license in order to drive. The beach is about a 20-minute taxi ride from the ship.

 Other than the 4-hour time commitment, the only real drawback is that you have two people per boat. It's more fun for the driver.

⚓ Adults: $88 (ages 10 and above)

Atlantis Submarine Expedition
(2.5 hours; Ages 4 and up)

Get a fish's-eye view of the colorful world under the sea, thanks to the U.S. Coast Guard-certified submarine *Atlantis*. As the sub dives 110 feet into the deep, guests see tropical fish and towering coral formations, while a narrator makes the wonder of it all even more wonderful. Once the boat surfaces, passengers will have yet another treat—free rum and fruit punch.

We met some parents who took their kids (ages 6 and 10) down under. They found it to be a kid-friendly experience. And although we enjoyed the tour, we recommend that claustrophobes avoid this one.

⚓ Adults: $99 (ages 10 and above)
Children: $57 (ages 4–9; must be at least 36 inches tall)

Clear Kayak and Beach Snorkel Combo
(2.5–3 hours; Ages 10 and up)

A visit to one of Cozumel's newest beach clubs, the exclusive Uvas Beach, includes a 45-minute guided kayaking experience, plus 40 minutes of spying on under-sea critters with provided snorkel equipment, and a chance to splash in the ocean, play in the sand, or snooze on the beach.

The kayak experience is not for wimps! We like having the choice of whether to snorkel or not to snorkel—since the allotted beach time (45 minutes) simply isn't enough for us.

⚓ Adults: $68 (ages 10 and above)

Cozumel Ruins and Beach Tour
(4–4.5 hours; Ages 5 and up)

Culture and leisure go hand in hand on this guided tour where you explore the ancient history of Cozumel at the San Gervasio Ruins, a Mayan religious center, and then chill out at Playa Mia Adventure Park for an hour and a half of swimming and water sports (there is an additional charge for equipment). The terrain is rough here, so strollers are not allowed. Beverages are included, and food may be purchased.

The terrain wasn't only too rough for baby strollers—it was tough for adult "strollers," too.

⚓ Adults: $52 (ages 10 and above)
Children: $35 (ages 5–9)

OTHER PORTS OF CALL

On special sailings, usually during the Christmas holidays, Disney Cruise Line adds a couple of destinations to its cruises. The trade-off (there always is one) is that you may have to sacrifice two of those leisurely sea days. But if these ports appeal to you, remember: These extra-special sailings only happen once or twice a year. Check with your travel agent for dates. Know that special cruises are very popular and tend to sell out far in advance. For information on upcoming special sailings, visit *www.disneycruise.com* or call 800-910-3659.

Ocean View Explorer Tour
(2 hours; All ages)

Look below! This glass-bottom boat lets you see underwater without getting your feet wet. Fish, other fascinating marine life, and colossal coral formations of Paradiso reef appear before your eyes. There's not a bad seat in the house—er, boat.

What We Think

If you absolutely, positively don't want to go into the water, this is a nice opportunity to spy on creatures of the deep.

⚓ Adults: $46 (ages 10 and above)
Children: $35 (ages 9 and under)

Dolphin Trainer for a Day
(5.5 hours; Ages 10 and up)

After a brief taxi ride, guests arrive at Dolphinaris, where they have the chance to enjoy up-close encounters with enchanting marine mammals. The day begins with a 50-minute primer on our flippered friends, followed by snack time— for the dolphins *and* the humans. After a 45-minute snorkel session, it's "face-to-flipper" time. You'll no doubt marvel as dolphins complete tasks at your command. For some, it's all about the belly ride. (Hang on!) Lunch is included.

What We Think

If you are a physically fit dolphin fan, it doesn't get better than this! It's a long day, but quite rewarding.

⚓ Adults: $285 (ages 10 and above)

Dolphin Kids at Dolphinaris
(3 hours; Ages 4 to 9)

After a kid-friendly intro to dolphins (including a discussion of anatomy, physiology, and history), guests experience a close encounter with Pacific bottlenose dolphins. Under the supervision of a trainer, children enjoy 40 minutes of interacting with the friendly mammals. The experience is capped with a little dolphin showboating (kisses, hugs, and jumps). Kids must be accompanied by a parent or guardian who sign up for the Dolphin Observer at Dolphinaris excursion (see page 125).

Thrilling for most youngsters, though some little ones might be a bit spooked by the up-close encounter with the enormous creatures. They may also get squirmy during the lesson. Older kids dig it.

⚓ Children: $105 (ages 4–9)

Dolphin Swim at Dolphinaris
(3 hours; Ages 5 and up)

Following a brief dolphin lesson, guests make their way to a submerged (waist deep) platform and enjoy an in-water exchange with real live bottlenose dolphins. You'll learn how dolphins respond to hand signals, get some hands-on time with the crafty mammals, and even share a kiss with one of your newfound friends (or a handshake for the modest). The bonding continues in the deeper coves area, where everyone is treated to a belly-ride, courtesy of our fine flippered-friends.

For us, 40 minutes of quality time with these magical creatures is priceless. Though the actual price is a bit hefty! Still, it's a gem of an experience.

⚓ Adults: $160 (ages 10 and above)
   Children: $145 (ages 5–9)

Discover Mexico & Chankanaab
(5 hours; Ages 5 and up)

Celebrating Mexico from the pre-Hispanic age to modern times, Discover Mexico is a cultural park brimming with exhibits for the whole family. Expect to spend about 75 minutes exploring this facility before moving on (via taxi) to Chankanaab National Park. This spot boasts more than 350 species of plants and is awash with tropical fish and colorful underwater vistas. Break out the snorkel equipment pronto! If that's not your thing, feel free to relax on the beach or set out on a nature walk. Lunch is included.

 Tackling two compelling parks in 5 hours is a tad ambitious, but still worthwhile.

⚓ Adults: $59 (ages 10 and above)
Children: $39 (ages 5–9)

Dolphin Push, Pull, and Swim
(3–5.5 hours; Ages 8 and up)

Cozumel offers plenty of dolphin fun, but this adventure adds another dimension—a swift ride on a boogie board while tethered to the pectoral flippers of a dolphin. The fun happens at Chankanaab National Park where you also can put on a mask and swim with the friendly dolphins —it's so easy to fall in love with these smart and graceful marine animals.

 Just climb on and ride—this is an easy, safe step beyond the belly ride offered with other Cozumel dolphin experiences.

⚓ Adults: $139 (ages 8 and above)

Four Elements–A Mayan Adventure
(7 hours; Ages 10 and up)

Are you physically fit and itching for an adventure? This seven-hour experience will whisk you to Chikin-Ha —a protected natural sanctuary—and immerse you in Mayan culture. Activities highlight primal elements of earth, water, wind, and fire. Expect to bike through farmlands, snorkel in natural limestone sinkholes, and even fly above the jungle (on a zip line). This excursion is best enjoyed by active folks. It's not for anyone with any physical limitations whatsoever.

 We admit it: We are just too doughy to get the most out of this experience. Daredevils and gym rats, on the other hand, more than get their money's worth.

⚓ Adults: $105 (ages 10 and above)

Dolphin Observer at Dolphinaris
(3 hours; Ages 3 and up)

This excursion lets water-wary guests observe friends or family as they "swim" with the dolphins. "Observers" are treated to the same overview of dolphins as those who swim with them, including their amazing history and underwater communication system. After that, they relax and watch loved ones interact with dolphins in a pool and ocean cove setting. Talk about a photo op! (This excursion may be booked in conjunction with Dolphin Swim at Dolphinaris, Dolphin Trainer for a Day, or Dolphin Kids at Dolphinaris.)

 We prefer dolphin encounters from anear (not afar!), but this is an ideal way to bond with loved ones as they bond with the sea mammals.

⚓ Adults and Children: $25 (ages 3 and above)

If you are fans of all things Disney but think that a Disney cruise might be too, um, cutesy for your taste, you might be surprised. Adult tastes and sensibilities are factored into the overall equation for the Disney ships. Sure, kids abound (they even have their own deck), but you have your own pool, restaurant, and spa. Come sundown, the over-18 set can mosey over to Route 66 (*Wonder*), Beat Street (*Magic*), or The District (*Dream*) —and enjoy a festive cluster of entertainment venues earmarked exclusively for grown-up guests.

At many ports of call, there are tours—scuba, snorkeling, golfing, and the like—where the under-18 crowd can't crowd you. In fact, on Castaway Cay, Disney's own private island, you can bask in the sun or read a novel in the shade of a magnolia tree on a beach designated especially for grown-ups. You can even have a massage in a private cabana overlooking the ocean.

After all, this is your vacation, and it's understandable that you'd expect some measure of privacy and more than a modicum of peace and quiet, and grown-up fun. And, of course, bingo.

Snuba Cozumel
(2.5–3 hours; Ages 10 and up)

If you love snorkeling and wish you were a certified scuba diver, this adventure lets you take the next step with fins, a diving mask, weights, and a breathing apparatus—but your air tanks are strapped to a pontoon raft on the surface of the beautiful turquoise waters. A certified dive master takes you into shallow water to practice breathing, then leads you to water about 15 to 20 feet deep. The sea life is astounding.

What We Think *You need to feel comfortable swimming in open water, but it's a whole new world when you can drift along submerged for about 25 minutes.*

⚓ Adults: $69 (ages 10 and above)

3 Reef Snorkel
(3.5–4 hours; Ages 8 and up)

After a 30-minute sail to the first snorkel spot, you'll get gear and a safety briefing. Then it's time to take the plunge and frolic with the fishes for another 30 minutes. Two stops and half-hour dips later, it's time to head back to the ship. Each guest gets a boxed lunch (sandwich and chips) and a beverage.

 If you simply love to snorkel, this is the excursion for you. For others, three reefs might be one (or two) too many.

⚓ Adults: $49 (ages 10 and above)
  Children: $39 (ages 8–9)

Adventure Park, Zip Line, & Snorkel Combo
(3–6 hours; Ages 10 and up)

They don't call this an adventure for nothing! The experience includes "zipping" across a wire that's 25 feet off the ground, navigating a suspension bridge, and scaling one of the 70 climbing routes in Cozumel's Adventure Park. You can cap off the land experience by rappelling from the high platform in the park. After that, you can enjoy a peaceful snorkel.

 We are 'fraidy cats, and thus spooked by the zip line. However, this one's quite a thrill for daredevils.

⚓ Adults: $75 (ages 10 and above)

GRAND CAYMAN

In 1503, when Christopher Columbus came upon these islands (there are actually three Caymans: Grand Cayman, at 76 square miles, is the largest; Little Cayman; and Cayman Brac), he named them *Las Tortugas*, a nod to the then-large turtle population here. The present name is closer to *caymanas*, the Spanish-Carib word for alligators, although the nearest relatives you'll find here are iguanas. What you *will* find are big bucks (the paper kind, that is). George Town, the capital city of Grand Cayman island, is one of the world's largest financial centers, home to more than 500 banks.

Of much greater interest to leisure travelers is that the sparkling waters off its Caribbean shores make Grand Cayman a snorkeler's and diver's dream. In fact, it's one of the top five dive destinations in the world. Waters teem with coral and fish, and even non-swimmers can get a view of these underwater wonders—including the Cayman Wall and its resident population of stingrays—from a glass-bottom boat or mini-sub.

Shoppers should head for Fort Street and Cardinal Avenue. *Note:* Although you may be tempted, steer clear of all items made from turtle and black coral. Both are endangered species. In fact, items made from sea turtle cannot be brought back to the United States. Opt instead for some of the interesting jewelry fashioned from shipwreck artifacts—some old gold pieces, perhaps? And if hunger strikes, have lunch in town. Our favorite island treat is conch (pronounced *konk*)—as fritters or in chowder. Trust us, it's delicious.

Sea Trek Grand Cayman
(1.5 hours; Ages 10 and up)

It's more than snorkeling, yet it's not quite scuba diving. Here guests get to explore the crystal-blue waters in a "helmet-diving" experience. The specially designed oxygen helmet lets you immerse yourself below sea level for a fun-filled, 30-minute guided tour. Though folks need not have a diving or snorkeling background, it helps to be in strong physical condition. (Expectant mothers, guests with heart or respiratory issues, and those with back or neck injuries can't participate.)

 We are flat-out fascinated by this helmet contraption. It allows all the joys of snorkeling without swallowing any of the sea! Can be a tad claustrophobic, though.

⚓ Adults: $89 (ages 10 and above)

Seven Mile Beach Break
(4 hours; All ages)

A short air-conditioned bus ride is all it takes to get to Grand Cayman's newest beach destination: Sea Grape Beach. So grab a lounge chair (no extra charge), a complimentary soft drink, sit back, relax, and enjoy. Take some cash along, as there's an opportunity to buy grilled snacks and other beverages. Water-sport equipment rentals are also available.

 A beach day we can get excited about! The transportation-beach time ratio is just right, as is the area of beach that's reserved for Disney Cruise Line guests. And the price is right.

⚓ Adults: $36 (ages 10 and above)
   Children: $26 (ages 3–9)
   Under age 3: free

Nautilus Undersea Tour and Reef Snorkel
(3 hours; Ages 5 and up)

Here's an opportunity to see the sea from both above and below. Onboard the *Nautilus*, the world's largest semi-submarine, you'll sail over some spectacular shipwrecks and out to Cheeseburger Reef. As for the "below" part of the adventure: Don your goggles and snorkel with the rainbow of tropical fish that call this home. Snorkel gear is included.

 "A nice day" was mostly what we heard about this tour. Folks expected more when they heard the word "Nautilus" (like deep dives and so on), but they generally enjoyed the time and felt it was worth the money.

⚓ Adults: $52 (ages 10 and above)
   Children: $43 (ages 5–9)

Pirate Encounter
(2.5 hours; Ages 3 and up)

This excursion could be called "We Wanna Walk the Plank!" A short tender-boat trip takes guests to one of the world's last wooden brigs, *Valhalla*. Friendly pirates are there to welcome you aboard, sail the ship past Seven Mile Beach, and make you walk to the plank (don't worry, you don't have to jump, but you should—it's a lot of fun!). Figure on about 40 minutes of splashing-around time.

 Who knew how much fun it would be to jump off the side of a pirate ship—again and again and again?! It's not for guests with limited mobility, but young'uns love the pirate factor.

⚓ Adults: $42 (ages 10 and above)
   Children: $28 (ages 3–9)

Stingray City Reef Sail and Snorkel

(3.5 hours; Ages 5 and up)

No mere dip-your-face-in-the-water-near-the-shore experience, this seven-mile adventure aboard a 65-foot catamaran gives you an opportunity to explore the deep, study the coral formations, and watch fish cavort before your eyes. All snorkeling equipment, water, and soft drinks are provided.

Members of our group went on this tour and gave it high marks. The snorkeling location for this one was peaceful, and a knowledgeable guide enriched the experience immensely. A good time was had by all—even the fish.

⚓ Adults: $60 (ages 10 and above)
  Children: $47 (ages 5–9)

Boatswain's Adventure Marine Park

(4.5–5 hours; All ages)

Turtles, lizards, and sharks—oh, my! You'll see them all at Boatswain's Adventure Marine Park. The shore-side retreat is home to more than 11,000 turtles at the historic Cayman Turtle Farm. There's also a 1.3 million-gallon lagoon that's teeming with wildlife. You may take a stroll down the Nature Trail (if you want to see those lizards), shop on Cayman Street, and/or dive into Breaker's lagoon. Snorkel equipment is provided, food is not (though it is possible to buy some).

It's a bit pricey, but you get a lot for the money. A must for turtle fans.

⚓ Adults: $92 (ages 10 and above)
  Children: $72 (ages 3–9)
  Under age 3: free

Seaworld Explorer Semi-Submarine
(1.5 hours; All ages)

Down periscope! It's time to submerge for a look at the treasures under the sea on this semi-submarine that takes you to two genuine shipwrecks and allows you to get an underwater view of an unforgettable array of sea life. Best of all, you'll have a marine-life expert onboard to give you some history and answer all of your questions.

What We Think

The shipwrecks were fun to look at, and the fish were simply fabulous. The guide made the history of the area come to life. A winner.

⚓ Adults: $43 (ages 10 and above)
Children: $31 (ages 9 and under)

NEW SHIP ON THE HORIZON

The Disney Cruise Line fleet is doubling in size! That's right, after the *Disney Dream* joins the family in 2011, the *Disney Fantasy* will soon follow (in 2012). The *Fantasy* will have 1,250 staterooms and, like its predecessors, boast a design reminiscent of the classic ocean liners of the 1930s (with Disney touches, of course!). For updates, visit *www.disneycruise.com* or call 800-951-3532.

HOT TIP

While ashore waiting for tours to gather, be sure to pick a shady spot where you can easily spot your group.

Atlantis Submarine Expedition
(2.5 hours; Ages 4 and up)

Have you ever heard of barrel sponges? Neither had we until we took this underwater tour aboard the *Atlantis XI* sub and saw them through the portholes (they're among the world's largest sponges). We also saw star corals, stingrays, turtles, and other exotic fish. Note that all guests must descend a ladder into the submarine. The tour is not recommended for guests with limited mobility or wheelchairs.

 We liked this one. Not only because it was like taking a course in Sponges 101, but the fish (we're suckers for stingrays) were the stars of the day.

⚓ Adults: $99 (ages 10 and above)
   Children: $57 (ages 4–9; must be at least 36 inches tall)

Nautilus Undersea Tour
(2 hours; All ages)

If *under* water isn't your thing, then try this very impressive alternative. The *Nautilus* glides like a boat and gives you a glorious underwater view like a sub, but never completely submerges. What's more, you get to view the deep (without actually going there) in a spacious, air-conditioned underwater observatory. Best of all, the wonders of life below come alive as a marine-life expert regales you with tales of the sea on this amazing tour of shipwrecks, sea life, and incredible coral reefs.

 "Great for landlubbers like us" is what we heard from folks who took this tour. The comfort level onboard was excellent.

⚓ Adults: $43 (ages 10 and above)
   Children: $31 (ages 9 and under)

Shipwreck and Reef Snorkeling
(2.5 hours; Ages 5 and up)

First stop is the *Callie*, one of the Caymans' most famous wrecks. Onboard, experienced dive masters provide a history of the ship plus give those who need it some instruction in snorkeling. The next stop affords guests the opportunity to view some spectacular coral reef formations and tropical fish; you may even spot a turtle. Snorkeling equipment, ice water, and lemonade are provided.

 This tour proved a major favorite among our scouts. They loved the snorkeling and the shipwreck—and one of them saw a huge turtle. Totally excellent, dude.

⚓ Adults: $39 (ages 10 and above)
Children: $31 (ages 5–9)

Rum Point Beach Adventure
(5 hours; All ages)

Life really is a beach on this day of doing absolutely nothing on a beach that affords you absolutely everything. Only a short bus and ferry ride away, Rum Point is *the* place to go for swimming, sunning, or relaxing. Tropical sound effects include casuarina trees rustling overhead. Sandwiches and beverages are included in this day of total indulgence. For more active folk, various water sports are available for an additional cost.

 The beach bums in our group thought this was the ultimate. So if you fall into that category, take note.

⚓ Adults: $59 (ages 10 and above)
Children: $49 (ages 9 and under)

WILL YOU MARRY ME—AGAIN?

Whether you're celebrating your first, fifteenth, or fiftieth, renewing your vows can be a life-affirming experience. Those couples who still feel like newlyweds long after the wedding day know that anniversaries can mark more than years. What better way to say "I love you still" than by having another wedding? Perhaps your first "I do's" were said in front of a justice of the peace; now you can don that white gown and do it up in grand style. Or, if you prefer to keep it low-key, a small corsage and boutonniere will do just fine. A ship's officer can perform the ceremony. Ask the kids along this time (chances are they weren't present for the first go-round), or make it a very private affair with just the two of you, as it was at the beginning. We can't tell you how many couples have decided to renew their vows on the Disney ships; suffice it to say that there's a lot of hand-holding, slow dancing, and stolen kisses to be seen on deck. For additional information, call (407) 828-3400.

Rum Point Beach Adventure and Stingray City Snorkel
(5 hours; Ages 5 and up)

Take the Rum Point tour described on page 135, add a glass-bottom boat ride to Stingray City where you can snorkel with the stingrays, and you know what we mean when we say, "Having it all."

 What We Think *We loved this relaxing beach day. And the snorkeling was cool, too!*

⚓ Adults: $95 (ages 10 and above)
Children: $82 (ages 5–9)

Grand Cayman Island Tour
(2 hours; All ages)

Although most folks head for the island's shores, the curious explorer should know that Grand Cayman is more than a beach—much more. And you'll discover this on an air-conditioned bus that meanders through the quaint streets of George Town and past the storybook-perfect gingerbread houses to the odd rock formations of the eerie island wonder called "Hell." Then it's on to the world's only turtle breeding operation of its kind, Cayman Turtle Farm.

 We were a little disappointed in this one. The turtles were interesting, but not worth the outing.

⚓ Adults: $39 (ages 10 and above)
    Children: $29 (ages 3–9)
    Under age 3: free

Island Tour and Snorkeling with Stingrays
(4.5 hours; Ages 5 and up)

A veritable smorgasbord of adventures, this tour lets you do it all in a scant 4 hours. First, it's a stop at world-famous Seven Mile Beach, then a chance to experience classic island architecture with a trip to Old Homestead, and, for nature lovers, a visit to the Cayman Turtle Farm. Naturalists will appreciate the island's prehistoric rock formation, a place the locals call "Hell." And last, but certainly not least, head to Stingray Sandbar to get up close and personal with sea life. Snorkeling equipment is provided.

 The turtle farm was just okay, but the snorkeling made up for it. You gotta love those stingrays.

⚓ Adults: $72 (ages 10 and above)
    Children: $56 (ages 5–9)

Aquaboat and Snorkel Adventure
(3 hours; Ages 10 and up)

Head for the high seas aboard a two-person inflatable motorboat, which you'll then pilot along Grand Cayman's scenic shores (there are instructors to show you how to maneuver the craft; "captains" must be 13 or older to drive and be accompanied by a parent or guardian 18 or older). Make a stop and explore the uninhabited Sandy Cay, just off the Cayman coast; then enjoy some R&R at Smith's Cove, a picturesque bay and secluded beach where you can swim, snorkel, or just chill on the sand. Well rested, you take the wheel again and head for the *Callie*, a submerged shipwreck, before returning to the dock and heading to Rackams Bar for a complimentary fruit or rum punch.

This was a banner day for most boat lovers who took the tour. Some parents didn't feel comfortable allowing their kids to pilot the boat, however. The scenery is amazing, and Smith's Cove was the icing on the cake. The shipwreck, we heard, was excellent, and the rum punch scored high.

⚓ Adults: $84 (per guest, with a maximum of two in a boat; ages 10 and above)

DISNEY'S NOD TO NATURE

In its ongoing attempt to maintain the integrity of the land and sea, the ecology-minded folks at Disney Cruise Line have taken the following steps:

⚓ Every sailing, the Disney ships recycle tons of aluminum, clean cardboard, and plastic.

⚓ Guests at Castaway Cay are urged to follow the "take only memories, leave only footprints" policy prohibiting the removal of shells—which are often homes for marine creatures—from the island.

⚓ Trans fat-free cooking oil that's been used in shipboard kitchens is combined with diesel fuel to power small vehicles, heavy equipment, and other machinery on Castaway Cay. This program helps reduce waste and the need to ship traditional fossil fuels to the island.

⚓ Mini-reefs are being cultivated in Castaway Cay's snorkeling lagoon to provide homes for small reef fish and invertebrates, and to encourage coral growth.

⚓ Many shore excursions include ecotourism components that benefit local communities and instruct tour guests on the wise use of natural resources.

⚓ More than 200 sea turtles have been nursed back to health and returned to their natural habitat by scientists at The Seas pavilion at Disney's Epcot theme park.

⚓ Dolphins, manatees, sea turtles, fish, and coral are some of the marine life protected and studied under the auspices of Disney's Worldwide Conservation Fund.

⚓ Each ship has its own Environmental Officer dedicated to environmental training, compliance, and waste management.

KEY WEST

The southernmost community in the continental U.S. and yet closer to Havana, Cuba, than it is to Miami, Key West is a charming blend of the best of southern, Bahamian, Cuban, and Yankee food, architecture, and hospitality.

Discovered (along with the rest of Florida) by Ponce de León, and a favorite destination of fishermen, artists, and writers, this tiny piece of land was home for 30 years to Ernest Hemingway (who, among other works, penned *To Have and Have Not* and *For Whom the Bell Tolls* here). President Harry Truman had his "little White House" here, and Tennessee Williams, John Dos Passos, and Robert Frost found these friendly climes ideal for their creative and leisure liking. In fact, travelers can still visit Hemingway's Spanish Colonial-style house and lush gardens, and Truman's Little White House Museum.

By all means, take the tour train or the trolley to orient yourself, but once you've done that, Key West is best explored on foot—stop and admire the architecture—from Bahamian wooden gingerbread houses to those of New England sea captains, complete with widow's watch. The oldest house in Key West, circa 1829, was owned by a sea captain; you can still tour it and see its ship models, furnished dollhouse, and seafaring documents. For shoppers, galleries and crafts shops abound, as do lots and lots of places to buy T-shirts. Or do what most everyone else does and take to the water—be it by glass-bottom boat, catamaran, or kayak.

Sail, Kayak, and Snorkel Excursion
(5 hours; Ages 10 and up)

Get the best of all wet worlds in this day of adventure off Key West's shores. A sail aboard a two-masted schooner takes you through some mangrove-shrouded islands; then it's off the sailing ship and on to paddle your own kayak on an hour-long trip through unspoiled natural surroundings. Finally, don your snorkel gear (provided at no extra charge; instruction included, too) to discover the undersea wonders of Florida's most popular key. Welcome back snacks include fresh fruit, chips, salsa, beverages, and more.

Ardent snorkelers have admitted to loving this experience, as well as most anything underwater; others were less enthusiastic, and would have preferred to have spent more time on the schooner.

⚓ Adults: $79 (ages 10 and above)

Back to Nature Kayak Tour
(3.5 hours; Ages 10 and up)

There's more to Florida than the beach. Climb aboard one of these double kayaks and paddle to the Wildlife Refuge; you'll be amazed at the number of (uninhabited) islands that are scattered along Florida Bay. You'll be in the company of a knowledgeable guide, who will point out the wildlife and the natural wonders and answer any questions you may have. It's like looking for pirate treasure—without having to walk the plank. At the end of the sail, you'll be treated to a soft drink.

 Nature lovers will truly enjoy this tour. Looking at a bird is fine, but having a guide tell you all about the bird and everything else you encounter makes this a wonderful—and peaceful—visit with Mother Nature.

⚓ Adults: $59 (ages 10 and above)

White Knuckle Thrill Boat
(2 hours; Ages 8 and up)

They don't use the term "thrill" lightly here. Expect one wild ride when you board a high-performance jet boat. Hold on tight! We're talking 360-degree spins, sudden stops, and wild slides. The fun is shared by you and up to 11 other riders. The half-hour of thrills is sandwiched by 20-minute bus transfers and 5-minute walks to and from the bus.

 The boat ride is fun, but the price is a little scary for a 30-minute experience. The free drink is a nice touch, but if you're craving snackage, you'll have to buy it.

⚓ Adults: $72 (ages 10 and above)
Children: $59 (ages 8–9)

Key West Catamaran Sail & Snorkel Tour
(3.5 hours; Ages 5 and up)

If you're the seafaring sort, this is the best way to experience the magic of Key West. You'll enjoy a 3-hour sailing adventure that includes snorkeling amid vibrant coral and tropical fish. Equipment and instruction are provided, as are beverages. Snorkeling is from the back of the catamaran in water that's about 15 to 20 feet deep.

 Good marks were given by all the guests who took this tour.

⚓ Adults: $49 (ages 10 and above)
Children: $28 (ages 5–9)

Pirate Scavenger Hunt
(Duration varies; All ages)

Avast, ye hearties, thar be a daily scavenger hunt a-happening at the Pirate Soul Museum, and you're invited to join in the fun. Guests reach the museum on foot (it's about a 10-minute walk) where they hunt solo or in groups (your choice). Guests who complete the hunt are rewarded with a swashbuckly bookmark.

 If you ask us, that is one expensive bookmark! But how often do you get to play in a pirate museum? For many kids, the mere idea of that is priceless.

⚓ Adults: $23 (ages 10 and above)
Children: $13 (ages 3–9)
Under age 3: free

Pirate Soul Museum & Shipwreck Historeum
(Duration varies; All ages)

Pirate enthusiasts step back in time and explore 17th-century Jamaica, where they gaze upon (and sometimes touch) artifacts and hear tales about the area's most notorious buccaneers. Energetic adventurers may ascend the 65-foot-high wrecking tower for a panoramic view of Key West.

Okay, so it's not Disney's Pirates of the Caribbean, but it's still cool. And the view from the tower is awesome.

⚓ Adults: $35 (ages 10 and above)
    Children: $20 (ages 3–9)
    Under age 3: free

Conch Republic Tour and Museum Package
(Duration varies; All ages)

Hop aboard an open-air train for a drive-by tour of more than 100 of Key West's main attractions and historical sites. Once you've had your orientation, you'll be provided with admission media for self-guided visits to the Key West Aquarium and the Key West Shipwreck Historeum Museum.

While the tour gives a nice overview of the island, there is no opportunity to hop off and explore your favorite sites (a bummer for some). Neither place earned raves from our crew. And our guide was gratuity-obsessed. Not cool. Though it was neat to see Ernest Hemingway's house.

⚓ Adults: $56 (ages 10 and above)
    Children: $29 (ages 3–9)
    Under age 3: free

Old Town Trolley or Conch Train Tour
(Duration varies; All ages)

Train or trolley? Take your pick—either one will take you on a 60-minute tour in the southernmost city in the U.S. Expect to see 100 local points of interest, including attractions and historical sites, such as Ernest Hemingway's house, the famous Sloppy Joe's, and more.

 We were a bit disappointed in this outing. First of all, the whirlwind pace left us frustrated. Why not a short stop at Hemingway's house, and how can they exclude the amazing Butterfly Conservatory?

⚓ Adults: $32 (ages 10 and above)
  Children: $16 (ages 3–9)
  Under age 3: free

The Key West Butterfly & Nature Conservatory with Aquarium
(Duration varies; All ages)

For those who crave serenity (now!), this excursion has your name on it. After a short walk and shuttle ride, guests enjoy a stroll through a tropical paradise. The climate-controlled environment is home to more than 50 species of butterfly, plus exotic and flowering plants, and cascading waterfalls. After the tour, guests are transported to the Key West Aquarium—the original tourist attraction in the Florida Keys.

We love this excursion. The Butterfly Conservatory is very interesting and serene. We overheard lots of "oohing" and "aahing" from kids and grown-ups alike. The aquarium delivers, too. They let you pet the sharks!

⚓ Adults: $43 (ages 10 and above)
  Children: $28 (ages 3–9)
  Under age 3: free

Glass-Bottom Boat Tour on the Pride of Key West
(2.5 hours; All ages)

Perfectly named, the *Pride of Key West* is a 65-foot, glass-bottom catamaran that gives passengers an incomparable view of the underwater world of the Keys. And comfort is key here, too: There are upper and lower sundecks, a large climate-controlled viewing area, and restrooms. A big plus is the narrated ecotour of North America's only living coral reef. Sit back, relax, and enjoy. Snacks and beverages are available to buy.

 Comfort with a capital C is the key word to this Key tour. And the narration was a major plus.

⚓ Adults: $42 (ages 10 and above)
   Children: $25 (ages 9 and under)

Presidents, Pirates, & Pioneers
(2 hours; Ages 3 and up)

Step back in time during this walking tour and discover the stories behind some of the city's most famous places, including the Shipwreck Historeum Museum and the Harry S. Truman Little White House. The tour concludes with complimentary conch fritters and bottled water. In all, expect to walk about 1.5 miles. Wheelchairs are permitted, but the Shipwreck Historeum is not wheelchair accessible.

 This is a nice way to soak up a bit of history and get some exercise to boot. Wear comfortable walking shoes! A good tour guide makes all the difference in the world.

⚓ Adults: $38 (ages 10 and above)
   Children: $23 (ages 3–9)

Key West Golf
(5–5.5 hours; Ages 10 and up)

The Key West Golf Club offers a full 18 holes of challenging golf, complete with the famous Mangrove Hole—a 143-yard, par 3 that is played over a field of tropical mangroves. You'll reach the club after a 20-minute van ride from the ship. Once there, grab some rental clubs, jump into a shared golf cart, and start swinging. (It's okay to bring your own clubs, but they must be inspected by U.S. Customs). The tour includes clubs, cart, and greens fees. Beverages may be purchased at the club house. Bring cash or a major credit card.

 When the weather's decent, serious golfers relish the chance to yell "fore!" in the southernmost city of the United States.

⚓ Adults: $189 (ages 10 and above)

GPS Walking Tour
(Duration varies; All ages)

If you love gadgets, this easy, mile-long walking tour is for you. You'll get your own global positioning system (GPS), and the tour starts just steps from the ship. At each destination, the GPS will give you fun facts about the city's most famous landmarks. Feel free to wander, because the handheld, electronic map always lets you know exactly where you are. End with a cold drink at Pat Croce's Rum Barrel.

 A fun way to learn a little Key West history, especially for first-time visitors.

⚓ Adults and children: $29 (ages 3 and above)
   Under age 3: free

Snuba Key West

(2.5–3 hours; Ages 10 and up)

What's *snuba*, you ask? Well, what's snuba with you?! It's actually a cross between snorkeling and scuba. Guests breathe through a scuba regulator that is connected to an air tank that's on a raft floating on the surface. It allows swimmers to stay underwater as long as they want (provided they want no more than 25 minutes) and venture as far as 20 feet deep. No certification is necessary, but participants must feel comfortable swimming in open water and be free of any health problems.

 Definitely an interesting twist on the traditional snorkel experience. A plus for us is that each group of six has its own dive master for guidance.

⚓ Adults: $109 (ages 10 and above)

Explore Key West by Electric Car

(Duration varies; All ages)

Key West is the perfect-sized city to discover in an electric car. A "Go GPS Ranger" will guide you on a route that starts on Duval Street and includes more than a dozen highlights, from the Hemingway House to Kermit's Key Lime Pie Shop. Video and audio pop-ups keep it fun. With three hours of car-time, you can stop along the way.

 An easy way for up to four people to see Key West's quirky sights.

⚓ Cost: $179 (per car; for up to 4 people)

Island of the Arts
(2.5–3 hours; Ages 14 and up)

Laid-back Key West is home to dozens of talented artists, and this is your chance to see some of the best. You'll peek into the homes and studios of two noted ceramic artists, then stroll through the Gardens Hotel, one of the prettiest in Key West, with unusual sculptures on the grounds. Next stop is The Studios of Key West in the old U.S. Armory, home to dozens of up-and-coming artists. Finally, you'll stop at the new Art Bar, where metal sculptress Barb Grob will fire up her torch for a demonstration. (And you'll go home with one of her signature metal geckos.)

 Most enjoyable if you love fun and funky art.

⚓ Adults: $119 (ages 14 and above)

Snorkel, Kayak, & Dolphin-Watching Adventure
(3.5–4 hours; Ages 5 and up)

A 20-minute boat ride deposits guests at Key West Wildlife Refuge—home to a vast array of marine life and small outlying islands. The adventure begins by paddling through winding mangroves. Next up? A shallow-water snorkel by a shipwreck (a remnant of 2005's Hurricane Wilma). Afterward, you'll head to an area known as the "Dolphin Playground." It's home to about 100 bottlenose dolphins. Have those cameras ready!

 The refuge is lovely, the snorkeling is swell, and spotting dolphins is the best! Of course, there's always a chance they'll be camera shy.

⚓ Adults: $95 (ages 10 and above)
  Children: $85 (ages 5–9)

President Truman's Key West
(2–2.5 hours; All ages)

Key West was President Truman's home away from home. To that end, he even had a "Little White House"—the beautifully restored starting point for this trolley tour. It's about a five-minute walk to the trolley (or train). Once aboard, you'll pass sites such as Ernest Hemingway's home and museum (and maybe spot an ancestor of his six-toed cats!), the Audubon House museum, and the schooner *Western Union*. In all, more than 100 points of interest are touched upon. It involves a bit of walking along the way, so wear comfy shoes.

This is an ambitious, but informative tour. We were fascinated by the history of the "Little White House," but wished we had more time to visit sites such as Hemingway's house. Young children are likely to get antsy during this often enlightening experience.

⚓ Adults: $46 (ages 10 and above)
Children: $25 (ages 3–9)
Under age 3: free

CASTAWAY CAY

If you've ever dreamed of getting away to a private, tropical island, the folks at Disney have made it easy to fulfill the fantasy. Castaway Cay is a tiny island in the Abacos, one in the string of Bahamian isles. This little patch of paradise was secured for the sole use of passengers cruising on the Disney ships. It's small—only 3.1 miles long by 2.2 miles wide—and nearly 90 percent of it was intentionally left undeveloped so that nature lovers can enjoy some still-unspoiled terrain.

Here you can take a ride in a glass-bottom boat or a fishing boat, go back to nature on a kayak adventure, try your wings at parasailing, or go snorkeling offshore—and then return to a barbecue feast. Of course, if you'd prefer to loll about in a palm-tree-shaded, beach-side hammock, refreshing beverage in hand, well, that can certainly be arranged.

Other island amenities include biking, beach games, organized activities for kids and teens, a shaded pavilion complete with billiards, ping-pong, basketball, shuffle-board, and more, Disney character greetings, plus a secluded, adults-only beach. The icing on the cake? How about an open-air massage in a private cabana overlooking the sea?

Souvenir hunters aren't forgotten either: One store sells items you can only find here (we once got a shirt that said it all: *Help me stay on this deserted island. No shortage of food or drink. Surrounded by crystal-clear water with fun things to do! Never want to go back to civilization. Please do not rescue me!*). Castaway Cay also has a post office, so you can tell the folks at home all about life on a private island.

Walking and Kayak Nature Adventure
(2.5–3 hours; Ages 10 and up)

Explore, learn, and take advantage of the island's natural wonders on this memorable adventure to the tranquil side of Castaway Cay. On the 40-minute walk to your kayak launch site you'll have your own personal guide to give you an inside look into the Bahamas' geology and history. Then you can work out your bi- and triceps on your one-hour kayak excursion through the ecologically sensitive mangrove environment. You'll even develop a sense of the importance of the mangrove ecosystem as a nursery for immature marine life and a habitat for birds.

As you stroke your oars through the shallow waters, you'll view a just-below-the-surface show starring tropical fish, sponges, and colorful coral formations. While you're there, enjoy a swim in the turquoise waters off a secluded sandy beach, where you may also explore the wonders of the seashore's tidal zones and their diverse vegetation. A 20-minute hike brings you back to your tram stop. A naturalist's nirvana, this tour is a must for the eco-minded among us.

This was a nice tour for nature lovers—the younger sailors in our crew enjoyed it most of all. Some of us (the lazy ones!) would rather have relaxed out on the beach, but if Mother Nature's masterpieces are your cup of tea, this is the place to enjoy them all.

⚓ Adults: $64 (ages 10 and above)

Glass-Bottom Boat Scenic Voyage
(1 hour; All ages)

This visit to the deep (without getting wet!) affords you a panoramic window to the world under the sea aboard a 46-foot, glass-bottom trawler. The hour-long narrated eco-tour gives passengers the skinny on what's happening down there. Best of all, the boat's expansive underwater windows provide a commanding view of the barrier reefs that protect Castaway Cay. It's fun to try and count the number of different types of fish, sea creatures, and coral you can spot during your journey.

What We Think

If you don't mind taking time away from the island, we thought this was an enjoyable experience. You do get a chance to see the island, look underwater and try to count the fish, and relax. If you are lucky enough to spot some dolphins and watch the guide feed them, it's more than worth your time; if not, well . . . that's in Mother Nature's hands, not ours. Our guide was great, very knowledgeable and friendly. Note: *Seating on the boat is limited, so you should be able (and willing) to stand for long periods of time. Babies (and those tending them) won't enjoy this one.*

⚓ Adults: $35 (ages 10 and above)
 Children: $25 (ages 9 and under)

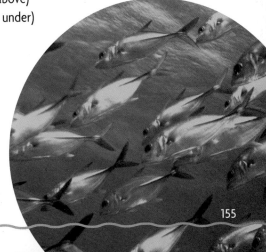

Sea Horse Catamaran Snorkel Adventure
(2–2.5 hours; Ages 5 and up)

Among the attractions of Castaway Cay are the colorful reefs that encircle it. Getting there really is half the fun, as a 63-foot catamaran whisks guests away to this snorkeling adventure. After receiving gear and a brief orientation, it's time to don those masks and dive in. Once you've dried off, enjoy complimentary snacks and beverages.

 If you still haven't had your fill of snorkeling, give it a whirl—although some snorkeling snobs thought the fish weren't as spectacular as those at the other ports.

⚓ Adults: $52 (ages 10 and above)
Children: $36 (ages 5–9)

Castaway Cay Bottom Fishing
(3–3.5 hours; Ages 6 and up)

This excursion gives guests the opportunity to enjoy the crystal-clear waters of the Abaco Islands while anchored for a fishing experience. Tackle and bait are provided, along with water and soda. Be sure to bring a hat, camera, and sunscreen—and expect to be joined by up to seven other fisher-folk.

 A new way to enjoy Castaway Cay, the fishing excursion gets a thumbs-up from enthusiastic anglers.

⚓ Adults and children: $117 (ages 6 and above)

Snorkel Lagoon Equipment Rental
(All day; Ages 5 and up)

You're on your own on this one: Pick up gear (at Gil's Fins and Boats) and put your face into the water of this 12-acre snorkel lagoon. Beginners can opt for Discover Trail, while more advanced water babies should follow the Explorer Trail. Snorkel awhile, rest on the beach, have some lunch, then snorkel some more—equipment rental is for the whole day. Snorkel, mask, fins, and vest are included. Kids under 13 must be accompanied by an adult at all times.

 Ideal environment for snorkel novices and small children. There's even an underwater Mickey Mouse statue to search for!

⚓ Adults: $25 for 1 day; $31.25 for 2 days (ages 10 and above)
Children: $10 for 1 day; $12.50 for 2 days (ages 5–9)

Watercraft Ski Adventure
(1 hour; Ages 8 and up)

What's it like to live on Castaway Cay? Here's your chance to find out. Board a personal watercraft and listen as a guide shares stories about the island's marine life, ecology, and storied history. Then it's off to a second destination, where your guide will describe the colorful history and environment of the Bahamas. Water shoes or sandals are the preferred footwear. Eyeglass straps come in handy, too. Note that riders board from the water—dress appropriately.

 Brief, but memorable. Lots of colorful photo ops. The boats are fun!

⚓ $95 for single riders; $160 for double riders. Guests must be age 8 or older to ride, 18 and up to drive, 16 with their parents' permission.

Float/Tube Rentals
(All day; Ages 5 and up)

If doing absolutely nothing sounds good to you, rent a tube or float and bob in the gently rolling waves of a lagoon. The water is crystal clear and, best of all, rentals are good for the whole day! Children under 13 years of age must be accompanied by an adult. Floats and tubes can be picked up at the family beach. (Grown-ups can also get them at Windsock Hut at Serenity Bay.) Don't forget the sunscreen.

What's not to love? Take it all in—soon you're back in the real world.

⚓ Adults and children:
   $6 for 1 day; $7.50
   for 2 days (ages 5 and above)

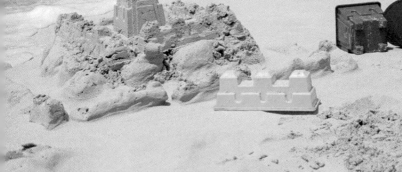

Parasailing

(45 minutes, airborne 5–7 minutes; Ages 8 and up)

On this once-in-a-lifetime experience, you get a high-flying view of the world around you as you soar approximately 600 to 1,000 feet above Castaway Cay. You'll enjoy a whole new perspective of the landscape—and the boats that look more like bathtub toys. Although the entire flight lasts only five to seven minutes, the preparation for the adventure and landing encompasses about 45 minutes. It's an experience you won't soon forget. A couple of restrictions: Guests must weigh more than 90 pounds, but must not exceed 375 pounds. Children under 13 must be accompanied by an adult. Non-flying guardians stay on the boat while each participant takes a trip into the sky. Note that this excursion takes place weather-permitting.

One member of our hardy crew—at the tender age of 65— recently took to the skies on this aerial adventure. Not only did she live to tell about it, she said it was one of the most exhilarating experiences she'd ever had. And she told us . . . and she told us . . . and she's still telling us. Others found the experience a little scary, but thrilling. It really feels as though you're flying, but it's so gentle that you aren't always aware that you're moving. "Memorable" was the word from all who had their heads in the clouds.

⚓ Adults and children: $79 (ages 8 and above)

HOT TIP

Keep your cameras and valuables dry with specially designed waterproof bags available from L.L. Bean, Magellan's, and other retailers.

Goofy's Sand Lot
(All day; Ages 13–17)

Just like the beach it borders, this high-energy area is zoned for teens only. Among the activities to be enjoyed here are tetherball and volleyball. The Sand Lot's convenient location— mere steps from the crystal-clear waters of the Caribbean—makes it easy for kids to cool off after heating up the court.

 How cool is it that teens have their own space on Castaway Cay? Here they can play beach games without being pestered by younger siblings.

⚓ Teens only: free

Bicycle Rentals
(1 hour; All ages)

Don your helmet and enjoy a two-wheeled tour of Disney's private island. Bikes are available for rent by the hour, and there are child seats available for the little ones. Children must be able to ride a two-wheel bike and are required to wear helmets.

 This was an excellent family experience for all. Little ones sat at the rear of grown-ups' bikes, while older children had their own bikes. The roads aren't the smoothest, but everyone said that it was a fun hour's diversion.

⚓ Adults and children: $6 per hour

HOT TIP

Shore excursions and specifics are bound to change in 2011. Visit *www.disneycruise.com* for updates and additional information.

Castaway Cay Getaway Package
(All day; Ages 5 and up)

For active folks who want to snorkel and bike about this Disney isle, here's an all-inclusive package that lets you frolic till your heart's content. You'll receive snorkeling equipment and float rental for the day, plus a one-hour bicycle rental. Kids under age 13 must be accompanied by an adult.

Since it's pretty much a given that you'll want to snorkel, float, and splash in the ocean, or pedal about the island, the only real question to ask yourself is: Will I (and my family) want to do all three? If the answer is an enthusiastic yes, then we say go for it!

⚓ Adults: $32 for 1 day; $40 for 2 days (ages 10 and above)
   Children: $16 for 1 day; $20 for 2 days (ages 5–9)

The Wild Side
(4 hours; Ages 13–17 on the *Dream*; 14–17 on the *Magic*)

Attention, teens! Here's an adventure designed exclusively for you. Venture into uncharted territory as you explore the wild side of the island where you can snorkel, bike ride, and sea-kayak on your own. No moms, dads, or baby brothers and sisters here.

What We Think — *The teens who came back from this trip had nothing but good things to say about it; it was a special time to spend with old friends and new, and enjoy some grown-up hours away from parents and siblings. Awesome!*

⚓ Teens: $35 (13–17 only)

Boat Rentals
(30 minutes; Ages 5 and up)

For those who can't get enough of the Bahamian waters, a variety of boats are available for rent at Gil's Fins and Boats. All craft are subject to availability. They can't be reserved in advance—it's all walk-up rental only. Children under age 13 must be accompanied by an adult. All prices are for a half-hour rental, per person:
Paddleboats: 2-seater, $8; 4-seater, $10. Sea Kayak: 1-seater, $8; 2-seater, $10. Aqua Fin: $15. Aqua Trike: $15. Hobie Cat: $18.

What We Think — *Your choice. It's all here. Paddle (or pedal) to your heart's content.*

⚓ Adults and children: $8–$20 per half hour (ages 5 and above)

Grouper Game Pavilion
(All day; All ages)

Need a break from the sun? We've got just the place for you—Castaway Cay's Grouper Game Room. Located near the volleyball nets and the sports beach, it is a *shaded* game room and recreation area where guests of all ages can play table tennis, basketball, shuffleboard, foosball, giant checkers, a game of pool, and more. Happy news for Mom and Dad: These are fun and *free* activities.

What We Think

A surefire hit with kids, we've noticed more than a few grown-ups enjoying themselves in these parts, too. Table tennis, anyone?

⚓ Adults and children: Free

Extreme Getaway Package
(All day; Ages 5 and up)

As with the Castaway Cay Getaway Package (see page 161), this is not for lazy beach bums. The all-inclusive deal lets you have it all (well, most of it!) in a single day. You'll receive snorkeling equipment and float rental for the day, a one-hour stingray encounter (courtesy of the island's own Castaway Ray), plus a one-hour bicycle rental. And, yes, there will be some time for you to snooze in the sun, too! Children under 13 must be accompanied by an adult.

Too much of a good thing? Nah. You simply can't get enough of Castaway Cay. We find this package "extreme"-ly enjoyable.

⚓ Adults: $54 (ages 10 and above)
   Children: $39 (ages 5–9)

Castaway Ray's Stingray Adventure
(1 hour; Ages 5 and up)

Get up close and personal with Southern stingrays in Castaway Cay's private lagoon. (Don't worry, they can't sting.) The guided encounter (a human "Ray" is your guide) includes a background session about these interesting sea creatures and snorkel instruction. The adventure culminates with a chance to feed, touch, and swim with the rays.

What We Think

We know every minute on Castaway Cay is precious, but this is an hour well spent. We'll play with the rays any day.

⚓ Adults: $35 (ages 10 and above)
   Children: $29 (ages 5–9)

NASSAU

Is it really better in the Bahamas? That depends on who you ask! Within this island paradise, you will find places to shop, swim, snorkel, sail, gamble, and sip a cool, refreshing beverage while looking out over a turquoise ocean. (Some say the shopping district is sensational, others find it uninspired—different strokes for different folks.)

Beaches are plentiful, but for those who like to venture beyond the sand, there are places here—where goats outnumber TV sets, where the roads are not-so-smooth, and the ferries are off schedule more than on—that take you to the "true" Bahamas, where Bahamians do their traditional dance (the *junkanoo),* and *goombay* music fills the air. This is where you can sample authentic island cooking (lots of grouper, lobster, conch, and johnnycakes) and take a turn at going local, if only for a few hours.

There are actually about 200 islands and some 2,000 cays (pronounced *keys*) in the Bahamas, all scattered across 100,000 square miles of the Atlantic Ocean. The adventures that are described on the following pages are available to you in Nassau, the island nation's capital. Aside from its divine diving, rich in shipwrecks, there is much more to see in the Bahamas—be it lush gardens and waterfalls, or Victorian mansions and 17th-century Georgian buildings. The good news is that, for the most part, the island's pride in its heritage is reflected in the way it is maintained.

167

Discover Atlantis
(2–5 hours; All ages)

This is the perfect place to put your imagination to work as you immerse yourself in the legend of the lost city of Atlantis. A 20-minute, narrated bus tour drops you off a short distance from the Atlantis resort. Here's where the real fun begins: A guided voyage through the Discover Atlantis attraction reveals a re-creation of the lost city and more than 120,000 fish representing 150 species. You will get an interesting look at life in the ocean's depths. Return bus transportation is included and available every half hour from 1 P.M. to 5:30 P.M. After this time, you will need to take a taxi (additional cost) back to the ship before departure.

NOTE: There's lots of walking involved with this tour. Wear comfortable shoes.

This was a tour that featured a little bit of everything—a lot of truth, a little fiction, and an informed guide who asked only that you bring along your imagination. But . . . some people felt that they could have done as well getting to Atlantis without an excursion.

⚓ Adults: $52 (ages 10 and above)
   Children: $35 (ages 3–9)
   Under age 3: free

HOT TIP

If you've got kids in tow, be sure to ask your tour director about potential pit stops *before* the tour begins.

Atlantis Beach Day
(4–7 hours; All ages)

Here's a full-day adventure that begins with a 20-minute bus ride through the historic area of Nassau's Paradise Island, where you'll be dropped off at the nearby Atlantis resort. Upon arrival, guests get a beach chair and towel and someone to escort them to a reserved location on the beach to bask in the sun and surf. Have lunch at the Dive In snack bar (coupon provided), and the day is yours to spend as you like. Enjoy gaming at the casino, shopping at a variety of unique stores, or visiting Discover Atlantis, a special marine habitat that's home to more than 120,000 fish representing 150 species. Return bus transportation is included and available until 5:30 P.M. After this time, you will need to take a taxi (at additional cost) back to the ship.

NOTE: This excursion involves extensive walking. Wear comfortable shoes. Use of the pools and waterslides is not included.

What We Think

As with the Discover Atlantis tour (page 168), this was a good way to learn about Atlantis and sea life, but on this tour you also have time to lie on the beach. Some people may be disappointed that many of the amenities of Atlantis were not included—especially access to the better part of the beach. One couple thought it would have been better to rent a room at the Atlantis for the day and get everything included. We think that's going a bit far, but as they say, different strokes . . .

⚓ Adults: $82 (ages 10 and above)
   Children: $55 (ages 9 and under)

Sunshine Glass-Bottom Boat
(1.5–2 hours; All ages)

If you prefer *viewing* the deep without getting *into* it, try this glass-bottom boat ride where you can get up close, though not too personal, with coral reefs, a seemingly endless variety of tropical fish, and other creatures of the sea as the boat sails the waters of Nassau Harbor. Before you depart, a guide will point out some of the more interesting sights around this historic port city. If the weather cooperates, you may get to see the shipwreck of the *Mahoney*, lying at rest on the far side of Paradise Island.

 We talked to some folks who took this tour because they wanted something tamer than the "in-water" activities being offered. They were not disappointed. Others found it too tame for their liking.

⚓ Adults: $26 (ages 10 and above)
   Children: $17 (ages 3–9)
   Under age 3: free

Catamaran Sail and Reef Snorkeling
(3.5–4 hours; Ages 5 and up)

The lush tropical reef you'll find at your destination is the icing on the cake for this half-day outing: The catamaran, complete with its shaded lounge and spacious deck area, takes you on a cruise through historic Nassau Harbor. If you can tear yourself away from the view, you will receive snorkel instructions (equipment is included) from the knowledgeable crew who, for your safety, also accompany you into the water.

 We give this one a big thumbs-up. The boat was small, the instructions were thorough, and the fish were plentiful —what more could one ask? Okay, the water was a bit chilly, but still . . .

⚓ Adults: $49 (ages 10 and above)
   Children: $34 (ages 5–9)

Caribbean Queen Snorkel Tour
(2–3 hours; Ages 6 and up)

The day begins with a narrated tour of Nassau's points of interest; once you have had your history lesson, you boat to a reef at Athol Island. Now it's time to don snorkel equipment (which is included), while receiving instruction before entering the water, for about an hour of open-water snorkeling. The area around the reef is rich with an awesome variety of aquatic flora and fauna, an undersea experience that should not be missed. A big plus: The boat is equipped with freshwater showers and modern dive ladders.

 Once again, our resident snorkelers raved about the underwater adventure—and the freshwater showers.

⚓ Adults: $37 (ages 10 and above)
Children: $27 (ages 6–9; children must be accompanied by a parent or guardian)

Blue Lagoon Island Dolphin Encounter
(4–4.5 hours; Ages 3 and up)

After a 30-minute voyage on a catamaran, you'll arrive at Blue Lagoon Island. Here, you'll meet dolphin trainers and take in a bit of Dolphin 101. After class, each student spends 20 minutes in a specially designed, 4-foot-deep pool. That's where they'll pet and "dance" with a bottlenose dolphin. There is an "observer only" alternative to this excursion. (It's for those who prefer to watch, not touch—good for those folks acting as guardians for younger guests.)

 Though not a traditional "swim with the dolphins" adventure, this is a rewarding experience.

⚓ Adults: $125 (ages 10 and above)
Children: $110 (ages 3–9; children must be accompanied by a parent or guardian)

Blackbeard's Cay Stingray & Beach Adventure
(4.5–5 hours; Ages 3 and up)

The population of the underwater "Stingray Adventure" will be glad to mingle with you on this combination tour. First, a boat brings you to Blackbeard's Cay, where the fun begins. The reason we call this a combination tour is that you can interact with these fascinating and friendly creatures and then unwind on the beach and enjoy lunch (sandwiches, chips, and soft drink; no extra charge) before heading back to the ship. Remember to wear swimsuits and sunscreen.

Stingray lovers that we are, we adore this tour. The area is beautiful, too. Relaxing on the beach afterward was a perfect ending to the day.

⚓ Adults: $49 (ages 10 and above)
   Children: $39 (ages 3–9)

Ardastra Gardens and City Tour
(2.5 hours; All ages)

Expect a little bit of this and a little bit of that on this nature-history tour. You'll visit the tropical Gardens of Ardastra, where you can see the world-famous marching flamingos strut their stuff, feed beautiful lory parrots by hand, and view the largest collection of Bahamian land animals in the world. Then board a bus for a narrated city tour. Stops include many of Nassau's historical points of interest, such as Fort Fincastle, the Water Tower, and the Queen's Staircase.

What We Think *For us, the best part of the day was feeding the parrots, but there's so much else to see that you may find yourself short on time when you get to them. The birds are very tame, and feeding them is great fun. The flamingo show is good, and here's where you get to have your picture taken—standing on one leg, of course. The staff is very friendly and knowledgeable, and the bus tour was interesting. The only downside: By the time we got back to the port, most of the souvenir stands were closed.*

⚓ Adults: $42 (ages 10 and above)
   Children: $29 (ages 3–9)
   Under age 3: free

Dolphin Trainer for a Day
(5.5–6 hours; Ages 10 and up)

The day begins with a 15-minute bus ride to the Atlantis resort, where you will be escorted (figure on a 15–20-minute walk) to Dolphin Cay. After a behind-the-scenes tour and a quick lesson about dolphins, lunch is served. Following a visit to the resident sea lions, it's finally time to meet some of our fine-flippered friends. Guests swim beside them while wearing snorkel gear and riding a power scooter. The experience is capped off with a customized, close-up dolphin encounter. Pucker up—you're sure to receive a big ol' dolphin kiss.

The price is hefty, but this is one memorable dolphin encounter. And the sea lion visit was a nice treat.

⚓ Adults and children: $420 (ages 10 and above; kids must be accompanied by a parent or guardian)

Atlantis Aquaventure
(5–8 hours; All ages)

The excursion begins with a 25-minute bus ride and an escorted walk (about 20 minutes) to the 63-acre water park at the Atlantis resort. Following a guided tour of an underwater aquarium, you're free to enjoy the waterslides, river rapids, pools, and more. Water bikes, kayaks, and snorkel equipment may be rented. A light lunch is included. You'll have access to a beach, shopping, and a casino, too. Guests must be at least 48 inches tall to ride the waterslides. Swim diapers are a must for babies.

Water park fans will not be disappointed (well, unless the weather is crummy). It's a bit of a splurge, but we're not complaining. (Yeah, we love water parks.)

⚓ Adults: $160 (ages 10 and above)
   Children: $110 (ages 3–9)
   Under age 3: free

Atlantis Dolphin Cay & Aquaventure
(6–8 hours; Ages 3 and up)

Take the tour at left and toss in an educational encounter with dolphins, and you have an idea of what this day is all about. Dolphin Cay is an 11-acre, state-of-the-art home to more than 20 of the lovable creatures. After a tour of the marine habitat, a guide takes you to Dolphin Cay and offers an overview of dolphin behaviors. Then it's time to don a wet suit and mingle with the majestic mammals. Expect to bond for about 30 minutes. Before your swimsuit has time to dry, you'll be making a splash at the Aquaventure water park.

If budget's not an issue, this is a great experience for the whole family. It's a long day, but a memorable one.

⚓ Adults: $295 (ages 10 and above)
Children: $245 (ages 3–9)

Blue Lagoon Sea Lion Encounter
(4–4.5 hours; Ages 8 and up)

Blue Lagoon Island—a 30-minute catamaran ride away—is one of the few marine mammal centers in the world to offer the opportunity to interact with sea lions. The experience includes a lesson about these gentle, intelligent animals and a 30-minute visit in a specially designed, waist-deep pool. After you hug your new friend good-bye, say hello to the bottlenose dolphins that live nearby. Food is available for purchase. All guests must be at least 38 inches tall to participate.

Sea lions can be quite affectionate. Who knew? This experience is a home run for animal lovers.

⚓ Adults and children: $99 (ages 8 and above; children ages 8–12 must be accompanied by a parent or guardian)

ST. MAARTEN

Some call it St. Maarten, while others insist it's St. Martin. And they're both right. During the 1600s, after centuries of battles over dominance, Spain bowed out and the deadlocked Dutch and French agreed to disagree and split this small island in half—well, not quite half: The French got 21 square miles and the Dutch, 16. (Legends abound as to why, but our favorite is that the two countries decided to claim their territory by conducting a race around the island and the French won.)

St. Maarten—the Dutch side of the island, and one of the world's only land masses owned by two countries—is the lively sector, while St. Martin—the bucolic French side, larger but more serene, attracts visitors who crave peace and tranquility—with some gourmet food thrown in for good measure. Both sides boast abundant beaches and sparkling waters. Shoppers enjoy Philipsburg's no-tax-on-imported-goods policy. Lots of shops are downright tacky, but with a little effort you can manage to part with some green stuff during your stay. And, of course, there's gambling. Casinos line the area by the pier, and most of the Dutch-side hotels offer games of chance. The French, meanwhile, have bouillabaisse and onion soup. So it's possible to swim anywhere, have a meal on either side of the island, and either go to a club in Marigot (the French capital) or play the slots on the Dutch side. Whatever you choose, the cards are stacked in your favor on this *très* continental isle.

Seaworld Explorer–Coral Reef Exploration

(2.5 hours; Ages 3 and up)

Here's your chance to spy on sea creatures without getting the least bit water-logged. A 45-minute voyage on the semi-submarine *Seaworld Explorer* lets guests *ooh* and *aah* at aquatic life in its natural habitat *and* when some of it's brought aboard the vessel, courtesy of a skilled diver/sea critter wrangler. Beverages are included, but you may want to pack a snack. Unfortunately, wheelchairs cannot be accommodated aboard the vessel.

What We Think

The commute-time to fun-time ratio is a bit lopsided for our taste. But if you fancy yourself a semi-sub fan, it just may make your day. Claustrophobes, however, should sit this one out.

⚓ Adults: $45 (ages 10 and above)
  Children: $29 (ages 3–9)

Golden Eagle Catamaran
(4 hours; Ages 5 and up)

The beautiful Caribbean is yours for the swimming—or snorkeling (equipment provided) or sunbathing—on a relaxing ride that concludes with pastries and an open bar.

What We Think
A pleasant way to pass the time in the Caribbean. It was very laid-back, and if that's what you yearn for, this is for you.

⚓ Adults: $82 (ages 10 and above)
  Children: $46 (ages 5–9)

Rib Boat Adventure
(4 hours; Ages 8 to 70)

After a high-speed ride on an inflatable rib boat, guests have some quality snorkel time at Creole Rock. That experience is chased with a visit to the picturesque village of Grand Case, where one can sip a glass of wine or soft drink and take in the view of the island of Anguilla. After an hour on a nearby beach, it's all aboard the rib boat for the return trip. Hang on tight! Guests should bring towels and beach necessities.

 Talk about fun in the sun! The speedy (and splashy) rib boat experience is indeed thrilling—though it's not for everyone.

⚓ Adults: $75 (ages 10 and above)
  Children: $55 (ages 8–9)

Island Drive and Explorer Cruise
(4 hours; All ages)

Here you can enjoy the best of all worlds, visit Simpsons Bay Lagoon and then board the *Explorer* for a half-hour cruise to Marigot, the island's French capital. Sightsee and shop, and then take the scenic return to Philipsburg, the Dutch capital, where you can do some more sightseeing and shopping. Too history-heavy? Not a bit. Expensive? Only if you can't resist the shopping scene. Let your budget—and your willpower—be your guide.

 This was interesting—if you're into learning about island history. If you'd rather hit the beach, look elsewhere. We loved the French side, although Philipsburg is not without its charms.

⚓ Adults: $47 (ages 10 and above)
  Children: $24 (ages 9 and under)

Twelve-Metre Regatta
(3 hours; Ages 12 and up)

On this exciting sail, the closest thing to being a participant in an America's Cup race, you can be as much a part of the crew as you like, or just sit back and enjoy while others do the work. "Crew members"—that's *you*—are trained in everything from trimming a sail, to punching a stopwatch to grinding a winch. It's so authentic that the fleet here includes the 1987 America's Cup winner, Dennis Conner's *Stars & Stripes US-55*. Sailing experience isn't required, but it can enhance your enjoyment of the trip.

If you love boating, don't miss this experience. Lots of group members actually participated in the working of the ship; others just sat back and watched. Your call.

⚓ Adults: $89 (ages 12 and above)

French Riviera Beach Rendezvous
(5 hours; All ages)

Orient Bay, called "the French Riviera of the Caribbean," is where lounging on your own specially reserved beach chair on a mile-and-a-half white-sand beach and enjoying lunch and cool drinks amid coconut palms and lush sea grapes is *de rigeur*. On the way to the beach, your guide will give you a brief history of the whole island—but this outing is really about the beach, the beach, and nothing but the beach. Note that nude or topless bathing may occur.

It's a beautiful beach—the sand, the gentle waves, the total relaxation.

⚓ Adults: $59 (ages 10 and above)
   Children: $40 (ages 3–9)
   Under age 3: free

Under Two Flags Island Tour

(3 hours; All ages)

As different as their European counterparts, the French and Dutch parts of this island are well worth exploring. Here's an opportunity to see the best of both worlds on a scenic narrated bus tour, which includes a stop at Marigot, the French capital, for shopping and exploring the local markets—or perhaps a coffee at a café?

What We Think

This was a good chance to see and learn about this bi-national island. Our guide was first-rate, and the air-conditioned bus was comfortable (try to get a seat up front; the views are much better). We enjoyed the French side of the island more than the Dutch side; the architecture is prettier, and the restaurants are excellent—though we steered clear of the cockfighting (yikes!). We did some shopping in Marigot. The open-air market is rife with island shirts and dresses, plus some jewelry and assorted souvenirs. If you're really into it, you can let the bus go and take a taxi back to the ship.

⚓ Adults: $22 (ages 10 and above)
   Children: $17 (ages 3–9)
   Under age 3: free

St. Maarten Island and Butterfly Farm Tour
(3.5 hours; All ages)

Originating in Philipsburg, this narrated bus tour offers stunning scenery and, best of all, a visit to a butterfly farm on the island's French side. Once you've had your fill of fluttery creatures, you can fritter away time in Marigot, where markets, cafés, and duty-free shops are at your disposal.

What We Think *An enjoyable experience, but many agree that it's a bit too long—definitely not worth four hours of potential beach time.*

Adults: $38 (ages 10 and above)
Children: $28 (ages 3–9)
Under age 3: free

See and Sea Island Tour
(3.5 hours; All ages)

Everything worth seeing on land and sea can be yours on this eclectic tour. The action begins with a narrated bus trip to the Grand Case area, during which you can appreciate the beauty of the landscape. The bus tour is followed by a trip aboard the semi-submarine *Seaworld Explorer*, which lets you spy on sea creatures. Finally, the day ends with a visit to the quaint French town of Marigot, where cafés and shopping abound.

This tour had its heart in the right place, but its timing was way off: too little time to do much of anything anywhere.

⚓ Adults: $55 (ages 10 and above)
   Children: $36 (ages 9 and under)

Mountain Top Downhill Rainforest Trek
(3.5–4 hours; Ages 8 and up)

Good walking shoes are a must for this half-day outing in the wild. Your guide will familiarize you with the wonders of the wilderness as you ride in an open-air safari vehicle on your way to the heights—by island standards—of Pic Paradise. Your reward? Breathtaking 360-degree views of St. Maarten and its seven neighboring islands. After that, it's time for an all-downhill trek into the depths of St. Maarten's only rainforest. The hike—which takes approximately two hours—covers ancient trails under the canopy of 200-year-old trees. Guests are treated to sights such as a long-abandoned sugar plantation and, quite possibly, monkeys, a mongoose or two, and more than a few iguanas. Guests should be in good physical condition to participate in this trek—it's not terribly strenuous, but it does involve quite a bit of walking over irregular, sometimes steep, terrain.

While the scenery is gorgeous, it was just too darn hot for us to get much out of the experience. We'll try it again during a cooler time of year. It's fun to search for monkeys!

⚓ Adults: $65 (ages 10 and above)
   Children: $58 (ages 8–9)

Mountain Bike Adventure
(3.5 hours; Ages 12 and up)

What is quite possibly the most fun on two wheels can be had coasting along St. Maarten's stunning shores. Biking is on- and off-road, and we guarantee the scenery won't disappoint. Rest time is at the secluded cove of Friar's Bay Beach, where you can swim and sun while sipping refreshing beverages before returning to the ship.

Bring lots and lots of water. This is the tropics, and, although the views are spectacular, it can be very hot. Rewarding our bodies by plunging into the water was pure nirvana.

⚓ Adults: $78 (ages 12 and above)

Tiki Hut Snorkel

(2–6 hours; Ages 6 and up)

The *Tiki Hut* is actually a boat. A floating lounge, if you will. One that will serve you food and drink (for a fee) in between dips into the calm waters of a sheltered cove. Snorkeling equipment and instruction are provided. Hourly tenders (water taxis) are available back to the ship or downtown. It's about a 15-minute trip.

We are drawn to the kitschy concept. A treat for grown-ups, it seems a bit splurgy for young kids—they are less likely to be charmed by the tiki-rific-ness and more likely to have their fill of snorkeling long before the six-hour limit.

⚓ Adults: $67 (ages 10 and above)
   Children: $47 (ages 6–9)

Afternoon Beach Bash Tour
(3.5–4 hours; All ages)

It takes about 30 minutes to reach Orient Bay by bus, but the payoff for your patience is about two full hours of fun in the sun on one of the Caribbean's best beaches. Fruit punch and rum punch are free-flowing (literally—there's no charge), while water-sport equipment, parasailing, hair-braiding, and massages are available for an extra charge. Food and additional beverages may be purchased at any of the full-service restaurants or beach bars. Note that nudity or topless bathing may be encountered.

All in all, an enjoyable beach day—and an excellent value. Not for the modest (see above note!).

⚓ Adults: $41 (ages 10 and above)
   Children: $22 (ages 3–9)
   Under age 3: free

ST. THOMAS/ST. JOHN

Among the world's most popular cruise destinations, these two islands—just 20 minutes yet a world away from each other—were discovered by Christopher Columbus in 1493, on his second journey to the New World. St. Thomas is a mere 32 square miles; St. John, its smaller sibling, is just 19 square miles.

St. Thomas has weathered its fair share of hurricane damage in the not-too-distant past but has bounced back in dramatic fashion. Rebuilt and revitalized, it has become a gathering spot for ships, large, larger, and largest (some might say too many), to drop anchor. Rightfully claiming to have one of the world's most beautiful beaches, it's a destination for that alone. Yet, there is more—much more—to the island than the beach. The duty-free shopping is possibly second to none, with the streets of Charlotte Amalie overflowing with jewelry shops and galleries; it's also a place to pick up such local island souvenirs as scrimshaw, sculpture, dolls, ceramics, and basketry. Actually, you could easily spend an entire day (or days) shopping here.

A short ferry ride away, St. John is the laid-back sibling, boasting hiking trails, more than three dozen white-coral sand coves, and replete with more flowers and ferns, butterflies, and birds than would fit into the best dreamer's imaginings. As you might imagine, nature rules here, and it is a kingdom anyone—bird or human—would be proud to call their own.

St. John Trunk Bay Beach and Snorkel Tour
(5 hours; Ages 5 and up)

Embrace the charm of St. John on this land and sea tour that shows off the splendor of Trunk Bay Beach. Whether you opt to sunbathe or snorkel (equipment provided), life is truly a beach here.

What We Think

It's as good as it gets. Having five hours to do just as you please is wonderful; the snorkeling was first rate, too.

⚓ Adults: $62 (ages 10 and above)
  Children: $37 (ages 5–9)

St. John Island Tour
(5–5.5 hours; All ages)

A scenic boat ride from St. Thomas brings you to the unspoiled island of St. John, where you board an open safari bus that tools around the island—including a stop at the Annaberg Ruins (with its abandoned plantation house and sugar mill)—and affords breathtaking views of neighboring islands.

We haven't heard great things about this tour. Most folks were wishing they were on the beach.

⚓ Adults: $55 (ages 10 and above)
 Children: $32 (ages 9 and under)

St. John Eco Hike
(5 hours; Ages 6 and up)

You'll put 1.2 miles on your tennis or hiking shoes as you march through the lush forests of Cruz Bay. Scenic Lind Point Lookout and Honeymoon Beach are on the tour, too. Happily, there's plenty of time for swimming before heading to the Caneel Bay Plantation.

This gets a big thumbs-up from all of us. The scenery was amazing, the swimming superb, and the plantation was an excellent end-of-day treat.

⚓ Adults: $69 (ages 10 and above)
 Children: $50 (ages 6–9)

Butterfly Secrets & Mountain Views
(2.5–3 hours; All ages)

After an hour-long scenic journey to St. Thomas's Mountain Top (complete with a photo op stop overlooking the lovely Magens Bay Beach and a visit to a souvenir shop), you'll immerse yourself in the wonderful world of butterflies. A guide will regale you with stories while hundreds of the colorful insects flutter about. Do not forget the camera. Wheel-chairs must be manual and collapsible.

 What's not to love about a swirling swarm of beautiful butterflies? The bus ride is a bit long, and we didn't need the shopping stop, but the butterfly farm certainly was special.

⚓ Adults: $39 (ages 10 and above)
   Children: $25 (ages 3–9)
   Under age 3: free

Magens Bay Beach Break
(4.5 hours; All ages)

Spend time enjoying the laid-back lifestyle of the Caribbean at St. Thomas's premier beach (in fact, it's considered one of the most beautiful beaches in the world), where you can swim and sunbathe (beach chairs are available on a first-come, first-served basis). Floats and water toys may be rented; beverages, snacks, and lunch items may be purchased. Water is free. It takes about 25 minutes to get to and from the beach (via bus).

 Beach bums like us delight over this glorious day of rest and relaxation.

⚓ Adults: $47 (ages 10 and above)
   Children: $37 (ages 3–9)
   Under age 3: free

Tortola Dolphin Encounter
(2–2.5 hours; Ages 3 and up)

A one-hour ferry-ride away, the island of Tortola is where you'll board a bus for an hour-long drive to Dolphin Discovery. After an orientation, each guest enjoys an in-water exchange with dolphins. Following the 30-minute meet-and-greet, a buffet-style lunch is served. Note that you will pass through immigration as you arrive and exit Tortola, so bring your passport. And the walk from the ship to the ferry is about 10 minutes—wear comfortable shoes!

It's a lot of traveling for a brief encounter, but all 30 minutes of dolphin-bonding are golden.

⚓ Adults: $188 (ages 10 and above)
Children: $162 (ages 3–9)

Tortola Dolphin Observer
(2–2.5 hours; Ages 3 and up)

Is a loved one taking part in the Tortola Dolphin Encounter (at left)? Would you like to tag along, take photos, learn about dolphins, and wave to the magnificent mammals from a nice, dry perch? Then this is the tour for you! Meant to be booked in conjunction with the Encounter, the Observer allows guests to accompany those participating in the Dolphin Encounter without getting wet.

The perfect way for an aquaphobe to participate in a dolphin-y day.

⚓ Adults: $129 (ages 10 and above)
Children: $101 (ages 3–9)

Butterfly Anytime
(All day; All ages)

Just a three-minute stroll from the pier (and your ship), this tranquil St. Thomas butterfly farm is pleasant for all ages (provided, of course, that you enjoy butterfly-watching). A friendly guide will help you discover the fascinating life cycle of the winged insect—from caterpillar to flying marvel. Don't be surprised if one of the hundreds of fluttering butterflies stops to perch on your head. And be gentle!

Butterflies are pretty. This is our preferred way to visit them (it's better than the tour on page 194).

⚓ Adults: $15 (ages 10 and above)
Children: $9 (ages 3–9)
Under age 3: free

Doubloon Turtle Cove Sail and Snorkel Tour
(3.5 hours; Ages 5 and up)

Ahoy, matey! You'll feel as though you've stepped back in time when you board the 65-foot schooner *Doubloon*. The treasures to be found on this sail from St. Thomas are the memories you get to take home with you. And at Turtle Cove at Buck Island, you'll also have time to snorkel (equipment and beverages provided).

Note that no food is served onboard, so take a snack (no fresh fruit). Our guide was meticulous in informing us about snorkeling, insisting that we wear life jackets and getting into the water with us to point out the giant sea turtles below. The captain sells souvenir Doubloon *T-shirts, so you might want to bring some cash.*

⚓ Adults: $58 (ages 10 and above)
Children: $35 (ages 5–9)

St. John Barefoot Sail and Snorkel

(4.5 hours; Ages 5 and up)

Best of land and sea, this excursion includes a scenic drive to La Vida Marina and a sail on the *Allure* to one of St. John's beautiful white-sand beaches. There's time for snorkeling (equipment is provided), swimming, and sunbathing—all that good stuff.

 People on this outing loved everything about it and had a hard time tearing themselves away from the beach.

⚓ Adults: $82 (ages 10 and above)
Children: $59 (ages 5–9)

St. Thomas Island Tour

(2.5 hours; All ages)

To fully absorb the natural beauty of the island, take this open-air (wear a hat for sun protection) safari bus ride—and be sure to bring your camera. Photo ops abound at almost every turn, especially when you reach Mountain Top, the highest point on the island.

 If you've never been here before, this is a great way to see the sights—and it's short enough to leave time for the beach at tour's end. Kids are welcome, but little ones should sit on a grown-up's lap while on the bus.

⚓ Adults: $39 (ages 10 and above)
Children: $24 (ages 3–9)
Under age 3: free

St. John Mini-Boat Adventure
(4.5–5 hours; Ages 10 and up)

A 45-minute ferry ride deposits guests at the island paradise that is St. John—two-thirds of which is national park. There, guests board mini-boats (two people per boat) and explore the bright blue waters. Along the way, guides will direct the mini armada toward two of the best snorkeling spots in the Caribbean.

What a wonderful way to see St. John! As always, the snorkeling was tops (though a bit pricey).

⚓ Adults: $99 (ages 10 and above)

Water Island Mountain Bike Adventure
(3.5 hours; Ages 10 and up)

Take a short boat ride to Water Island (off St. Thomas) and enjoy the beauty of the area from the seat of a mountain bike. There's a stop at the beach for swimming and relaxing after your two-wheel adventure.

It's a nice bike tour, but not necessarily worth $72.

⚓ Adults: $72 (ages 10 and above)

Sea Trek Helmet Dive at Coral World Ocean Park
(3.5 hours; Ages 10 and up)

How does a leisurely, underwater stroll sound to you? Impossible? Not here. All it takes is a Sea Trek helmet, gloves, and special water shoes (and $89)—and presto! You're ready to meander among marine life at Coral World Ocean Park—the number-one tourist destination in St. Thomas. The underwater part lasts about 45 minutes and is followed by 90 minutes of free time to explore the park.

Definitely a unique underwater exploration. There is an abundance of sea life to marvel at.

⚓ Adults: $89 (ages 10 and above)

Golf at Mahogany Run
(6 hours; Ages 10 and up)

Golf pro wannabes will delight in this outing. The scenic, 18-hole, par-70 St. Thomas course was designed by George and Tom Fazio. It may be tough to concentrate on your game, as the amazing views almost cry out for a camera. Greens fees, a golf cart, and transportation are included; rental clubs are available for an extra charge.

Both casual and passionate golfers agree that this course is on a par with the best.

⚓ Adults: $275 (ages 10 and above)

Certified Scuba in St. Thomas

(4 hours; Ages 12 and up)

If you're scuba certified (and can prove it), dive right in! Explore the beautiful waters of St. Thomas on this two-tank dive that goes to a reef with a maximum depth of 60 feet, and a shallower second dive, usually to a shipwreck. Equipment, professional supervision, and transportation are provided; wet suits are not included.

 Our resident scuba diver raved about this adventure. Everything went smoothly, the shipwreck was a treat, and he emerged as enthusiastic as when he submerged.

⚓ Adults: $109 (ages 12 and above; guests under 18 must be accompanied by a parent or guardian)

Discovery Scuba Diving

(4–4.5 hours; Ages 12 and up)

You wanna scuba dive, but don't have certification? You've come to the right place! Don't worry—it's not as reckless as it sounds. The day starts with a lesson in how to use scuba equipment in shallow water and the "dive" takes place in a protected marine sanctuary where the water is no deeper than 40 feet. No experience is necessary, but guests must be physically fit and strong swimmers. Wetsuits may be rented for an additional $10.

 If you've ever wondered if scuba diving was for you, this is a great way to test the waters.

⚓ Adults: $105 (ages 12 and above)

Captain Nautica's Snorkeling Expedition
(3.5–4 hours; Ages 8 and up)

A swift speedboat ride from St. Thomas Harbor will take you to some of the most spectacular coral formations and abundant sea life in the Caribbean. Get personal with schools of colorful fish and sea turtles at two prime snorkeling spots: Turtle Cove at Buck Island and Little St. James Island. Light snacks and beverages are provided (for you, that is, not the fish).

Our snorkel volunteers enjoyed every minute of this expedition.

⚓ Adults: $75 (ages 10 and above)
   Children: $60 (ages 8–9)

Skyride to Paradise Point
(Duration varies; All ages)

Scenic views of St. Thomas abound aboard this 700-feet-high-in-the-sky tram. (Have a camera ready at all times.) Once you reach the top, you can enjoy the shops, nature trail, and cafe on historic Flag Hill. The skyride operates daily from 9 A.M. till 3 P.M.

An enjoyable way to travel provided that you are not afraid of heights. And the price is reasonable.

⚓ Adults: $18 (ages 13 and above)
   Children: $9 (ages 6–12)
   Under age 6: free

Screamin' Eagle Jet Boat
(1 hour; Ages 5 and up)

A 700-horse-power turbo-charged jet boat whisks guests through a scenic tour of the St. Thomas Harbor and along the coastline at breathtaking speed. Hold on tight—the 45-minute ride is anything but smooth. Guests must be at least 48 inches tall to experience the *Screamin' Eagle* jet boat.

 Very exhilarating! A real scream! Not for the faint of heart—or those wishing to stay dry.

⚓ Adults: $49 (ages 10 and above)
Children: $39 (ages 5–9)

Buck Island Catamaran Sail & Snorkel
(3.5 hours; Ages 5 and up)

Guests spill onto the fore-deck, sunbathe, sip a complimentary beverage, and enjoy a 40-minute sail to Shipwreck Cove. Once there, the captain drops anchor and it's fin-and-goggle-donning time. The 90-minute snorkel session takes place over a sunken shipwreck.

 We are always up for a sailing/snorkeling combo. And in this case, the shipwreck is an excellent bonus.

⚓ Adults: $52 (ages 10 and above)
Children: $32 (ages 5–9)

Kayak, Hike, and Snorkel of Cas Cay
(4–4.5 hours; Ages 8 and up)

Travel by van to the Virgin Islands Eco Tours Marine Sanctuary and explore its lush, tropical ecosystem aboard a two-person kayak. Guests also visit a hermit crab "village," and explore a marine tidal pool and a geologic blowhole along a coral beach. The capper is a beginner-rated, guided snorkel adventure.

 If you're fit as a fiddle, this active experience can be exceptionally rewarding. The sanctuary is beautiful.

⚓ Adults: $79 (ages 10 and above)
Children: $59 (ages 8–9)

Coral World Ocean Park by Land and Sea
(3.5 hours; All ages)

Okay, so the semi-sub may be a mere 8 feet underwater, but the views are truly depth-defying. The adventure lasts about 45 minutes. Then you're free to spend 90 minutes exploring the marine conservation park on your own. Highlights? The Deep Reef Tank, Stingray Pool, and a three-story *underwater* observation tower.

 The park isn't St. Thomas's most famous tourist attraction for nothing. If you're not claustrophobic, there are big thrills to be had.

⚓ Adults: $56 (ages 10 and above)
Children: $42 (ages 9 and under)

LAND AND SEA VACATIONS
Pairing a Disney Cruise with a Walt Disney World Vacation

It's the ultimate surf-and-turf experience for Disney fans— a Walt Disney World vacation that's paired with a Disney Cruise. (What better way to chase the Pirates of the Caribbean attraction than by visiting the Caribbean?! *Sans* real pirates, of course.) And, as ships are added to the fleet (the *Disney Dream* in 2011 and the *Disney Fantasy* in 2012), "land and sea" opportunities are limitless. The chapter that follows focuses on Walt Disney World. Why? For starters, a book that covered all of the real-world destinations would be, well, *enormous*. Plus, we've spent decades amassing vast amounts of Walt Disney World expertise —so it makes perfect sense to share it!

If you've been to Disney's world before, you know that it is not a small one. In fact, it covers 40 square miles. That's nearly twice the size of Manhattan—and with about as many attractions, restaurants, and places to stay as one might expect from an area that size. There are four theme parks, two water parks, two dozen hotels, a dining, shopping, and entertainment district, championship golf courses, boating, fishing, tennis, and more. Add a cruise to the mix, and even seasoned Disney veterans run the risk of becoming overwhelmed.

The good news is that a customized vacation package can include just about every-thing you'd ever want. That frees you up to focus on an important goal: having fun.

Land and Sea Packages

One of the most popular ways to experience a Disney vacation, this package pairs a stay at a Walt Disney World resort with a cruise aboard the *Disney Dream* or the *Disney Magic*. While land-sea package particulars were correct at press time, changes are in store for 2011. Call 800-951-3532 or check *www.disneycruise.com* for updates and package options.

Whether you do the land part of your trip before or after the sea leg, you'll have a choice of Walt Disney World's wide variety of resorts. Expect your digs to be comparable with the category of stateroom you select on the ship. That's to say, each hotel is in a certain category based on overall value. Disney Cruise Line can pair them up with comparable stateroom categories to ensure a seamless transition. A big plus to a package is the one-time check-in (for U.S. citizens). That means once you've checked into your resort, you'll have completed the check-in process for the ship, too—and you'll get to breeze by the check-in desk at the port terminal (don't forget your valid passport). In fact, the powers that be are so intent on making the transition from a Disney resort to the ship seamless, that the key to your hotel room does double duty as your stateroom key (except for the Swan and Dolphin resorts). This special card is known by insiders as the "Key to the World." Keep it with you at all times. (As with all details, this is subject to change.)

If you have cruise-related questions while at Walt Disney World, know there is a Cruise Line information desk in many Disney resorts. Check with the lobby concierge for specifics.

WHAT'S INCLUDED? WHAT'S NOT?

Quite simply, all Walt Disney World Land and Sea packages include accommodations on land (at a WDW resort) and a stateroom on a Disney ship. In addition to accommodations, shipboard meals, snacks, soft drinks, and entertainment come with all packages.

What's not included in base packages? Meals and beverages at Walt Disney World, transfers to Port Canaveral (although these can be purchased in advance), airfare, shore excursions, meals ashore in ports of call (with the exception of Castaway Cay), gratuities, laundry or valet services, parking, or any other items not specifically included.

What can be added? Just about everything. Options include tickets to Disney World theme and water parks, dinner shows, and more. Call 800-910-3659 for details.

HOT TIP

Disney Cruise Vacations offers a day-before option at a non-Disney resort with some packages. For information, contact a travel agent or call 800-910-3650.

Walt Disney World Resorts

Many of the 20-plus Walt Disney World properties hold the distinction of partnering with Disney Cruise Line as part of a land-sea vacation experience (For a complete listing, turn to page 214). We've stayed at all of them and can vouch for each and every one. What follows is a sampling of resorts from which you can choose (for details on WDW resorts, visit *www.disneyworld.com*, or grab a copy of *Birnbaum's Official Guide to Walt Disney World 2011*).

Animal Kingdom Lodge

The zebras, ostriches, and Thomson's gazelles out back are not escapees from the nearby Animal Kingdom theme park. They and their hoofed and feathered comrades live on the resort's carefully plotted pasturelands, giving round-the-clock credence to its claim as Florida's only African wildlife reserve lodge.

Romance and adventure cling to every richly appointed inch of the semicircular lodge, which serves as a five-story animal observation platform and boasts animal-viewing parlors, stellar restaurants, and an expansive swimming pool.

LOCATION: Animal Kingdom area
BIG DRAWS: Luxury laced with an undeniable spirit of adventure and romance. Amazing animal encounters.

Beach Club

This setting conjures up such a heady vision of turn-of-the-century Nantucket and Martha's Vineyard you'd swear you smelled salt in the air. Surely, architect Robert A.M. Stern's evocation of the grand old seaside hotels has the gulls fooled. The resort stretches along a picturesque shoreline complete with a swimming lagoon, lighthouse, and marina.

LOCATION: Epcot area
BIG DRAWS: The exceptional swimming area is second to none. Some of the World's best restaurants. Easy access to Epcot and Disney's Hollywood Studios.

DISNEY CRUISE VACATIONS AIR PROGRAM

If you plan to fly to Florida, consider allowing the Disney Cruise Vacations Air Program help you make the arrangements. In addition to lining up round-trip airfare for your whole party, they will secure motor coach ground transportation and baggage transfers. The service is available in more than 150 cities throughout the United States and Canada. For details, call 800-910-3648. At press time, this service was not included in the price of any of the vacation packages—but that may change.

Caribbean Beach Resort

In this colorful evocation of the Caribbean, the spirit of the islands is captured by a lake ringed by beaches and villages representing Barbados, Martinique, Trinidad, Jamaica, and Aruba. Each village is marked by clusters of two-story buildings that transport you to the Caribbean, with cool pastel facades, white railings, and metallic roofs. Old Port Royale houses eateries and shops.

LOCATION: Epcot area
BIG DRAWS: Excellent value. Cheery environs with a decidedly Caribbean feel. Kids love the pirate-themed pool.

Grand Floridian Resort & Spa

A romantic slice of Victorian confectionery, this resort recalls the opulent hotels that beckoned high society at the turn of the 20th century. The Grand Floridian's central building and five guest buildings—white structures laced with verandahs and turrets and topped with gabled roofs of red shingle—sprawl over acres of lake-side shorefront. Every glance embraces towering palms, stunning lake views, and rose gardens.

The impressive lobby features immense chandeliers, stained-glass skylights, and live piano and orchestra music. The resort also offers some of the best restaurants on Disney property.

LOCATION: Magic Kingdom area
BIG DRAWS: The height of luxury with a view of Cinderella Castle. And it's just one monorail stop away from the Magic Kingdom.

211

Polynesian

This resort echoes the romance and beauty of the South Pacific with enchanting realism. Polynesian music is piped throughout the lushly landscaped grounds, which boast white-sand beaches, torches that burn nightly, and sufficient flowers to perfume the air.

Guest buildings, which are set amid tropical gardens, are named for Pacific islands. But the resort's centerpiece is unquestionably the Great Ceremonial house, which contains a three-story garden that all but consumes the atrium lobby.

LOCATION: Magic Kingdom area
BIG DRAWS: A breathtaking, you-are-there South Seas ambience makes the "Poly" exceptionally romantic. It's connected to the Magic Kingdom via monorail and water taxi. And the volcano pool is a huge kid-pleaser.

Port Orleans Riverside

Southern hospitality takes two forms at this resort: pillared mansions with groomed lawns, and upriver, rustic homes with tin roofs and bayou charm. The Sassagoula River curls around the resort's main recreation area like a moat. Bridges link guest lodgings with this area and the steamship-style building that houses the resort's eateries.

LOCATION: Downtown Disney area (near Epcot)
BIG DRAWS: Exceptional value. A lovely setting.

Port Orleans French Quarter

New Orleans's historic French Quarter is evoked in this resort's prim row house-style buildings, which are wrapped in ornate wrought-iron railings and set amid romantic gardens and tree-lined blocks. Guestrooms are located in seven three-story buildings. The whole enclave is set alongside a stand-in Mississippi River, known as the Sassagoula.

LOCATION: Downtown Disney area (near Epcot)

BIG DRAWS: A good bang for the buck. Charming environs. It's the least sprawling of the moderate resorts. And kids get a big kick out of the pool area and serpent slide.

Saratoga Springs Resort & Spa

Long for the relaxation of a lake-side retreat—complete with fragrant gardens, bubbling fountains, and a spectacular spa? Look no farther. This resort has all of the above, plus colorful Victorian architecture, rolling hills, and even a classic boardwalk. The property aims to recapture the charm and rejuvenating ambience of Saratoga Springs, New York, circa the late 1800s.

LOCATION: Downtown Disney area (near the Marketplace)

BIG DRAWS: A soothing spa and lovely pool area (zero-depth entry). A 10-minute stroll to the Downtown Disney entertainment district, this resort is a Disney Vacation Club property (but available to everyone).

Walt Disney World Resort Options

The following is a comprehensive list of Walt Disney World resort hotels that participate in Disney Cruise Line's Land and Sea package program. The information was correct at press time, but is subject to change. In addition to WDW, it's possible to book vacation packages that pair a cruise with a hotel stay in Barcelona, London, Vancouver, and other destinations. For additional information, visit *www.disneycruise.com*, or call 800-951-3532.

DELUXE:
Animal Kingdom Lodge
BoardWalk
Contemporary Resort
Grand Floridian Resort & Spa
Old Key West
Polynesian Resort
Saratoga Springs Resort & Spa
Wilderness Lodge
Yacht & Beach Club

MODERATE:
Caribbean Beach Resort
Colorado Springs Resort
Port Orleans—French Quarter
Port Orleans—Riverside

VALUE:
All-Star Movies
All-Star Music
All-Star Sports
Pop Century

GROUND TRANSFERS

Disney Cruise Line provides reliable, friendly service aboard its motor coaches (aka: buses). Getting to the buses is easy. Upon arrival at Orlando International Airport, take a tram to the Main Terminal. Once there, proceed to the Disney Welcome Center. It's on Level One, Side B. Look for Disney's Magical Express. The real bonus here is the baggage handling: Disney reps will pull your tagged luggage and make sure it gets delivered to your room. This applies to the land-sea vacation package travelers, too—provided that they've purchased their package through Disney Cruise Line. From the airport, a bus will take you to Port Canaveral or a WDW hotel. (For guests with transfers included in their cruise package, your bus departure location and information is included in your cruise documentation.) What if you're staying at a resort that's not designated as a departure location or at an off-property hotel? You'll have to get yourself to one of the WDW departure spots to catch the bus to the boat! Here's a rundown of pricing for ground transfers:

TRANSFER TRIP	PRICE*
Airport to select WDW resort (one-way)	Free**
Select WDW resort to Port Canaveral	$35
Round-trip from Orlando International Airport (MCO) to Port Canaveral	$69
Land and Sea package (Orlando airport to select WDW resort; WDW resort to Port Canaveral; Port Canaveral to airport)	$69

*Prices are per person, were correct at press time, and are subject to change.
**Transportation from Orlando International Airport to WDW resorts will remain free throughout 2011 (and beyond). It is provided by Disney's Magical Express.

Walt Disney World

Whether you plan to spend three days or three weeks, chances are you'll have a tough time taking in all of Walt Disney World. The vast resort boasts four theme parks, two water parks, four spas, championship golf, boating, waterskiing, tennis, fishing, parasailing, horse-back riding, stock-car driving, and much more.

If your time is limited to a few days, we recommend visiting the theme parks and taking in the best attractions they have to offer (see pages 219–220). If you have the luxury of time, we suggest you stagger your visits to the parks, and intersperse peaceful respites by the pool, sporting activities, and shopping sprees. In any case, you'll also want to treat yourself to a classic Disney dining experience, even if it's simply an ice cream bar in the shape of you-know-who's head.

Theme Park Tickets

The process of selecting a ticket to Walt Disney World theme parks can leave your head spinning more than a ride in a teacup. To simplify the process, ask yourself a few questions: How many days will I spend in the parks? Do I have a favorite park? Will I be making another trip to WDW this year? If you've got one day only, you should buy a one-day "Magic Your Way" base ticket. That will allow you to visit one theme park for one day. Easy, right? Now, if you're going to be spending two or more days in the theme parks, it gets a bit trickier. You can purchase a multi-day (from 2- to 10-days) base ticket and customize it. Would you like to park hop? That is, to visit more than one theme park on one day? You should purchase the park-hopping option. Do you plan to visit

HOT TIP

Many multi-day tickets can be purchased by phone or via the Internet; call 407-824-4321, or visit *www.disneyworld.com*. There is a $3 handling fee, but it's convenient to arrive with tickets in hand. Allow at least three weeks for delivery.

a water park during your stay? Perhaps a trip to the ESPN Wide World of Sports complex, WDW's Oak Trail golf course, and/or Disney-Quest (Downtown Disney arcade)? Consider adding the "Water Park Fun & More" option to your base ticket. Finally, if you might not have a chance to use all of the theme park days allotted by the ticket, ask for the "no expiration" option. This is a kind of insurance. It allows for a little more spontaneity during your trip, since you won't be obligated to use up your entire ticket. That said, if you don't spring for the

"no expiration" option, *any unused days on the ticket will expire 14 days after it is first used.* No exceptions.

And last, there's the subject of an Annual Pass. What's that? You don't live in Florida, so how on Earth could this be worthwhile? The truth is, a premium annual pass costs about the same as a 10-day Magic Your Way ticket with all of the available bells and whistles. And, like the latter, it also includes admission to the water parks and Disney-Quest—plus a year of theme park admission. Annual passes net the bearer many discounts, including reduced resort rates.

Customized land and sea vacation packages may include 1- to 5-day Magic Your Way Tickets with Park Hopper Option. (Guests who customize their vacations themselves should customize their tickets accordingly.)

WDW RESTAURANT ROUNDUP

Walt's world is full of family-friendly dining establishments. Taking into consideration theming, value, and overall quality, these are some of our top table-service choices:

- Biergarten (Epcot)
- Boma—Flavors of Africa (Animal Kingdom Lodge)
- Cape May Cafe* (Beach Club resort)
- Chef Mickey's* (Contemporary resort)
- Cinderella's Royal Table* (Magic Kingdom)
- 50's Prime Time Cafe (Disney's Hollywood Studios)
- Garden Grill* (Epcot)
- Rainforest Cafe (Animal Kingdom and Downtown Disney)
- T-Rex: A Prehistoric Family Adventure (Downtown Disney Marketplace)
- The Wave . . . of American Flavors (Contemporary resort)

*Disney characters are in attendance for at least one of the meals offered by the eatery.

HOT TIP

To book a table at a WDW restaurant, call 407-WDW-DINE (939-3463) up to 180 days ahead. Call to confirm it before you leave home!

A Whirlwind World Tour

No matter how long you plan to stay at Walt Disney World, deciding what to do first can be a challenge. When it comes to the theme parks, if we had four days, we'd visit them in this order: Magic Kingdom, Epcot, Disney's Hollywood Studios, and Animal Kingdom. Since the Magic Kingdom is our favorite (and tops with most kids), we'd be sure to hop back to it once or twice. When it comes to narrowing the list of theme park "must-sees" to the barely manageable, we recommend the following attractions and shows that we believe stand head, shoulders, and ears above the rest.

MAGIC KINGDOM*

- Splash Mountain
- Space Mountain
- Big Thunder Mountain Railroad
- Pirates of the Caribbean
- The Haunted Mansion
- Peter Pan's Flight
- Mickey's PhilharMagic
- Buzz Lightyear's Space Ranger Spin
- It's a Small World
- The Many Adventures of Winnie the Pooh
- Wishes (fireworks show)

*With young children: Dumbo the Flying Elephant, The Many Adventures of Winnie the Pooh, Mickey's PhilharMagic, It's a Small World, Cinderella's Golden Carrousel, Tomorrow-land Speedway, Walt Disney World Railroad, and The Country Bear Jamboree.

EPCOT*

- Soarin' (Living with the Land pavilion)
- Spaceship Earth
- Test Track
- Turtle Talk with Crush (The Seas pavilion)
- Mission: SPACE (the less-intense, non-spinning version)
- IllumiNations: Reflections of Earth (fireworks show)
- The American Adventure
- Ellen's Energy Adventure (Universe of Energy pavilion)

*With young children: The Seas with Nemo & Friends, the Image Works play area in the Imagination! pavilion, Mexico's boat ride, and Kidcot Funstops in World Showcase.

DISNEY'S HOLLYWOOD STUDIOS*

- Toy Story Mania!
- The Twilight Zone™ Tower of Terror
- Rock 'n' Roller Coaster
- Block Party Bash
- Beauty and the Beast— Live on Stage
- Muppet*Vision 3-D
- Star Tours
- Fantasmic! (a combination fireworks/stage show)

*With young children: Voyage of the Little Mermaid, Muppet*Vision 3-D, Honey, I Shrunk the Kids Movie Set Adventure, Playhouse Disney, and Beauty and the Beast— Live on Stage.

HOT TIP

As the definitive source of insider information, we highly (and immodestly) recommend *Birnbaum's Official Guide to Walt Disney World 2011.*

ANIMAL KINGDOM*

- Expedition Everest
- Dinosaur
- Kali River Rapids
- Kilimanjaro Safaris
- It's Tough to be a Bug!
- Festival of the Lion King
- Pangani Forest Exploration Trail
- Maharajah Jungle Trek
- Finding Nemo—the Musical
- Flights of Wonder

*With young children: The Oasis, Festival of the Lion King, DinoLand, The Boneyard playground, Maharajah Jungle Trek, Pangani Forest Exploration Trail, and the Kilimanjaro Safaris.

INDEX